T0193679

FATHER ADAMS

BASED ON A TRUE STORY

NICK ADAMS

BALBOA.PRESS

A DIVISION OF HAY HOUSE

Balboa Press books may be ordered through booksellers or by contacting:

Balboa Press
A Division of Hay House
1663 Liberty Drive
Bloomington, IN 47403
www.balboapress.com
1 (877) 407-4847

Because of the dynamic nature of the Internet, any web addresses or links contained in this book may have changed since publication and may no longer be valid. The views expressed in this work are solely those of the author and do not necessarily reflect the views of the publisher, and the publisher hereby disclaims any responsibility for them.

The author of this book does not dispense medical advice or prescribe the use of any technique as a form of treatment for physical, emotional, or medical problems without the advice of a physician, either directly or indirectly. The intent of the author is only to offer information of a general nature to help you in your quest for emotional and spiritual well-being. In the event you use any of the information in this book for yourself, which is your constitutional right, the author and the publisher assume no responsibility for your actions.

Any people depicted in stock imagery provided by Getty Images are models, and such images are being used for illustrative purposes only. Certain stock imagery © Getty Images.

Print information available on the last page.

Interior Image Credit: Nick Adams / Fr. Mike Cross

ISBN: 978-1-9822-4526-9 (sc)
ISBN: 978-1-9822-4527-6 (e)

Balboa Press rev. date: 04/14/2020

I would like to dedicate this book to my children, Aaron Adams and Sara Adams. I hope God grants them many adventures and experiences. I pray God's spirit can touch them along the way. I love them both, dearly.

CONTENTS

FOREWORD

I feel that I provided not only the background for Nick's book but also the title, Father Adams.

I took Nick to dinner one evening at one of my favorite restaurants. We were greeted at the door by the owner, Talal.

"Good evening, Father Cross. We have your table all ready."

I was quick to introduce my guest. "Talal, I want you to meet my friend, Father Adams."

Talal always offers me a complimentary drink after I'm seated. It's part of the ritual when a man of the cloth patronizes his restaurant.

"Father Cross," Talal proceeds to ask, "may the house buy you and Father Adams a drink?"

"That would be nice, Talal," I answered.

"Thank you."

Talal took our orders, and then Nick questioned, "Why did you call me Father Adams?"

I replied, "You are a father. You got two kids to prove it. Besides, we got two free drinks out of it!"

I became acquainted with Nick Adams back in 1979. I had just arrived at St. Joseph's Church in Capitola, California, as a new pastor. My predecessor, Monsignor John Kennedy, had just finished building a beautiful new church, and it was debt free. What a break. I had no longer put my feet on the ground, however, when parents started asking me if I was going to do anything for the youth in the parish – like hiring a youth minister.

At this time, I knew Nick only as a reader at one of the Masses. Yet, he struck me as being a very devout Catholic, polite and quite knowledgeable of the faith.

He was a good reader and seemed to enjoy his part in ministry. Being a close friend to Monsignor John Kennedy, I decided to ask his opinion of Nick to learn a little more about Nick and his family.

Well, did I ever get an earful from Monsignor, who was extremely complimentary of Nick. When I told Monsignor that I was interested in recruiting Nick into youth ministry, Monsignor gave him nothing but high marks.

As time went on, I became more acquainted with Nick. I was fascinated by his pleasant personality. We even started a little socializing with one another. My first seven years in the priesthood was in campus ministry, working with young college people and running Newman Centers. So I felt well qualified in my discernment of Nick. He apparently had all the qualifications I was looking for; a pleasant personality, the right temperament, and a keen sense of responsibility.

So one day, I raised the question to him; "Nick, would you like to hired as our new youth minister?"

The answer that came back to me was a big unequivocal "Yes!"

We sent Nick to the Emmaus training program for potential youth ministers, conducted by the Archdiocese of San Francisco. It was a yearlong course, if I remember correctly. I can still recall how proud I was of him when I attened his graduation.

Nick was now officially trained and certified to take charge of our youth program. In our particular situation at St. Joseph's, he had to actually start the program from scratch; and that he did in no uncertain terms. Nick was a Pied Piper. The kids flocked to him, and their parents were overwhelmed by their kids' enthusiasm and interest in the church. Nick made it all happen. Our youth program was the envy of all the other parishes. Hiring Nick was the best thing I ever did for that parish community.

As time went on, Nick became very much in the saddle of activity. He never seemed to tire from making himself available to the young teenagers and devising activities that kept them coming to church and becoming a vital part of our parish community. He was quite imaginative, as I discovered; and, like most young people in those days, he had a thing for playing the guitar. Some of the tunes he played were of his own composition. Nick was a very exciting person to be around – really positive, if you know what I mean. You really never knew what was going to come out of him next.

My second love in life was flying airplanes. I had been flying at this time for about ten years and had earned an instrument rating. I also was a co-owner in a new four-place Piper Cherokee Archer 180.

I was putting plans together at that time to make a flight to Baja California in the late summer (1980). I had flown across the country on several occasions, but never to Mexico. It was also my plan to do some deep-sea fishing out of La Paz. I was told that mahimahi were plentiful in that area. It was my practice, on all my cross-country flights, to take someone along just for the company. They help keep me awake on those sometimes very long and boring legs of a cross-country flight!

After putting the trip together, I decided to ask Nick if

he would like to venture out of Capitola and see a little more of the world. Little did I know the guy had never been in an airplane all his life, not even a commercial one. Wow, was he ever going to have a "first time in my life" experience, not to mentiona real test of his very strong faith in God and – I guess one might say – faith in me too!

You're going to enjoy Nick's book, Father Adams, and how he uses his imagination, enthusiasm, and wit to keep you on the edge of your seat. I'm very happy to have played a not-too-small part in its production. After all, I did get us both back home safe and sound ---- eventually!

Father Mike Cross

THE BEGINNING

Where's my plane?

What was I thinking? The date was August 4th, 1980. I had agreed to accompany my parish priest on a vacation to Baja California. When he first asked me to go it sounded like a chance of a lifetime. Father Cross was a Catholic priest and a pilot: a very interesting combo. He intrigued me. He had an awkward sense of humor but lousy timing. We were attempting to fly his propeller plane from Watsonville, California all the way to the bottom of Baja California, Cabo San Lucas. "Piece of cake," is what Father Mike Cross called it.

My mother, a Portuguese fireball, was begging me not to go. She was always ready to inject her own opinions, feelings, and concerns; no matter the cost. She owned the last word like lake-front property. The guilt she could generate; like slow acting venom, found ways to penetrate deep under my skin. I knew this routine all to well. She had to tell me how this trip was hurting her! It was in her nature. One week before departure she let me have it,

"Do you know what this trip is doing to me?"

Before I could speak she tumbled on, "I won't sleep. I probably won't be able to eat. Come on, have you thought this through? People die in small planes; and believe me that is a

1

small plane. Two seats? Come on! You are my only son! Can't you see how this will affect me? It's almost torture to me."

Finally, a chance to speak, "Come on mom. Cabo San Lucas, La Paz, fishing and flying. Besides I am going with a priest. If we die; I should end up in purgatory."

My mom smiled at my attempt at a joke and returned, "I worry about the plane, is Father a good pilot? Do you trust him? You're putting your life into his hands. What does your girlfriend say?" I had run out of patience. Full steam ahead, "I am going mom. I understand what I am getting involved with. My girlfriend wants me to go; I want to go and I wish I could have your blessing too!"

My mother was incredibly religious, asking for her blessing went right to the heart of the matter. She melted, "Of course you have my blessing. You have my love and my blessing. Someday, you will know what this feels like. I am a worry wort; can't help it. I will be praying the whole time you're gone. I just wish you weren't going." She had to have the last word. We hugged and went over the rest of the travel plans.

Next week came too fast. The ride to the airport was unusually quiet. We were meeting people who would see us off. I had a couple of friends who wanted to see the plane. I hadn't seen the plane either so I was excited about casting my eyes on it. Of course my mom was with us and Father Cross had parishioners from the church join us too.

I felt invincible. I was 21 years old and at the top of my game. No fear. No consternation. Full speed ahead. However, when we arrived at the airport to get on Father Mike's plane; it wasn't even there! Where was the plane? Good organizational skills have always impressed me: being on time, balancing work and play, time management. Father Mike's plane wasn't even at the airport. I tried to stay calm.

Father Cross apologized to me and my mom and all our friends who had come to see us off. He was embarrassed; you could tell; so was I. He hurriedly made some quick phone calls. The trip was not off to a good start. One of my friends asked, "How well do you know this guy? I mean, Father?"

I lifted my shoulders and shrugged. This was all a bit odd. I started to get dirty looks from my mom and felt all the concern in the room. In fact, my mom pulled me aside and asked, "Nick? Where the hell is his plane? Are you sure you want to do this?" She had such a fake smile.

"Calm down mom." I nodded my head up and down.

The trip was planned, hotels booked, excursions (fishing) reserved. Too late to back out; though those thoughts were starting to surface. "Mom, it will be okay I'll ask Mike what's going on."

My mom glared at me and scolded, "You mean Father Cross! Don't be disrespectful to the priest, honey." My mother was old school, Catholic. Pre Vatican II. By the book.

I hustled over to Father Cross and met him as he was finishing up a conversation on the phone. He nervously explained, "Good news. My partner is flying the plane here now. Should be here in 30 minutes. He flying from San Jose. Some engine problem delayed him."

"Engine Problem!" I gasped.

Mike tried to calm me down, "Everything's okay. Glad they caught it before we took off." Mike joked.

Usually, I liked Father's sense of humor but not this time. At this point, not any of this as funny. Still, we were friends, and I came back with my brand of humor, "Swear, everything's okay with the plane Mike." I turned serious. "Swear it!"

"Nick, relax. The plane doesn't fly unless it's right. I will get a full diagnostic from my partner. For now, I'm buying everyone lunch." Mike finished and pushed me toward our friends.

Father Cross explained the situation to everyone. He apologized and assured all that the plane was fit and ready for the adventure before us. Father Cross blessed our food and maybe it was better that we all had a meal together before our departure. It had a calming effect. He also asked a special blessing on his plane. I faked a laugh. The emotion was suddenly starting to hit me. I could hardly swallow my food. Everyone looked for Mike's plane to land and when it finally did, I realized, this was really going to happen.

I grabbed my bags and headed out to the plane; everyone followed. Father Cross raced in front of us and opened the side door of the plane. He shook hands with his partner and engaged him in conversation. He motioned me to get ready. No turning back now.

I kissed my mom and gave hugs to all my friends. Mike, switched into the pilots seat, as his partner slowly walked away from the plane. We all waved our good-byes and before I knew it I was strapped into the seat next to Mike. I tried to show him some confidence. I gave him a thumbs up sign that I was ready. I had confidence in Mike. Hundreds of hours of practice and two trips across the United States gave him my respect. The take-off; my first in a small plane was perfect.

The sensation of flying is multiplied in a plane this small. You can feel the shaking. You can feel the torque. After take-off, I had a floating anxiety that invaded my body. I would have to find a way to relax; and soon. We planned twelve takeoffs and hopefully twelve landings. Still the views were beautiful. I could see everything below. us. This helped me relax; at least enough to enjoy the ride. I really had no other choice.

Honestly, I had no idea the sensations my body would

experience. The plane's propeller was less than five feet from my face! If that stopped, we would cease to exist. My brain had carefully repressed all thoughts of what could go wrong. The engine was human made, with flaws only know to the mechanics. Was Mike really honest about the engine? How often does this plane have engine problems? The plane had one hundred eighty horsepower, a cruising speed of 125mph, twenty four gallons of fuel and a ceiling of 7,500ft.

The vibrations of the torque on the engine made my senses work overtime. My ears heard the rotors spinning and my body felt the sonic vibrations all through the seat. Waves of constant shaking penetrated my skin deep down to the bones. Looking out at the propeller, I never realized it spun so fast. You could feel its energy and power. It moved the plane easily. The other problem with flying in a small plane is the outside inertia. Trade winds, clouds, air pockets, wind sheer, and rough weather had no problem moving our plane; sometimes knocking it right out of the sky. I instantly noticed we could drop ten feet without notice. We could also rise ten feet straight up. Being pushed left and right from cross winds also added to all the variables that a pilot would have to encounter. No one had to tell me to keep my seat belt on. The fasten seat belt sign would be "on" for the entire trip. I constantly checked my belt to make sure it was tight. Small air shifts could knock us around pretty good.

After the first hour I started to relax; at least, play brave. Mike would apologize for the sudden shifts and remind me to keep my belt on. He would move the plane higher or lower to smoother air. Sometimes, he found some stable air, sometimes he didn't. I was adapting. I would be on high alert; but trying to have fun.

The first day of the trip was uneventful; the second was not.

HAVE YOU EVER LANDED ON A DIRT FIELD?

I shoved the binoculars so tight against my eyes tears dribbled down my cheeks.

Pressing the glass against my skin left circular traces embedded on my tender skin. My eyes ached from the pressure and desperately searched for the runway that could save our lives. We were 1,000 feet high and being filled with pure adrenaline. The ground offered us no safety; no place to land. It was on our map, a small red plane signifying an airport or runway. However, in reality, invisible to our eyes.

Frustration crept in as we remembered planning the trip and double checking all landing sites and runways. Anger swelled up as we realized that we might have screwed up. Was this some sort of trick? But I know I felt mostly fear; people die in small planes.

Where was the courage.? Our plane was a Piper, Cherokee 180, single engine, low wing plane. We were running on fumes; we had to land and refuel the plane. The gas gauge was still above empty but it was almost touching the bottom line.

We were running out of options. We could both see the runway on the map but it was a whole different story on the ground. San Felipe, a small town in Baja California had no airport, no runway, no tower, no communication or buildings. Nothing. I tried not to panic as I glanced at Mike my pilot. He looked worried, yet totally focused. He tried not to show me his anxiety but he couldn't hold it back. I knew we were in trouble. "How much time do you think we have?" I asked.

Mike said, "Don't worry. We can land on the beach if we have to. We will find it. It has to be there. It's right on that damn map. I have buddies who have landed here."

I have never heard Mike swear before. Damn was a curse word for Mike. Mike was Father Mike Cross. A Catholic priest, who invited me on this trip. He was also my pilot and called the trip an adventure.

I called it a vacation but whatever it was now pushing both of us into an uncomfortable zone. Being at the mercy of such a sophisticated mechanical devise was both exhilarating and aggravating. Suspense and danger cancel out vacation. We were trying to fly the plane from Watsonville, California, all the way down to the tip of Baja, Cabo San Lucus. It sounded so cool. A test; carefully planned, with a need for some trust and courage. I don't know if I trusted Mike because he was a Priest or because he seemed to be a good pilot. I wasn't sure I had the courage to take on this sort of adventure. People die in small planes all the time, I was only 21. I wanted to roll the dice and take some chances but I wasn't ready to die yet. In fact, this wasn't what I signed up for. This pushed me way beyond my comfort zone. Why had I agreed to put myself in such a risky situation?

My thoughts were out of control. I suddenly saw a red shimmer of cloth waving briskly by a small grove of trees. A small red wind sock blowing east and through the trees and on the backside of the grove; a runway.

I shouted, "I see it! Holy Cow I see it!"

Father Mike said," Alright you did it. I'll fly over and take a look."

We flew over it once and from my uneducated view it looked magnificent. Long and lot's of room between two rows of trees; a piece of cake. We started our second fly by and Mike got a little closer to the ground but didn't touch down.

I started the questions: "Aren't we going to land? What's up?"

Mike didn't look happy. Anxiety had invaded his body. The stress was squeezing him tight. Sweat poured from his forehead. I could hear him breathing and his upper lip was a lake. He stuttered, "Have you ever landed on a dirt field?"

I sat speechless. I had never flown in a small plane before so, of course, I had never landed on a dirt field. I answered, "What do you mean a dirt field? How do you know?"

"It's dirt alright, Mike lectured, "Maybe sand, I don't know how packed it is. Don't worry I can do this but the plane could slide; we just can't let her flip over."

He sounded confident, yet he looked so stressed. I questioned, Mike have you ever landed on a dirt field?"

"No not really. But I have buddies who beached their planes before. Heck, we have a runway and I don't think we have a choice."

Every second was important. We started in Watsonville and to play it safe, we knew every four hours we would have to land and refuel. Our four hours were almost up. The gas gauge was now ever so close to touching empty. My central nervous system was now in full flight; heart rate up, breathing up, blood pressure up, a flood of sweat pouring off my nose dripping on my drenched shirt.

We headed for final approach. We both knew this was it. I tried to be calm as Mike needed confidence. Our wheels were just inches from the dirt when Mike kicked the engine into high gear and did another fly over. I was going crazy. "What's wrong! Land the damn plane our fuel has only minutes left."

"I can't tell what that runway is packed with. Notice there are no other planes or buildings. This runway could have been abandoned years ago. I didn't see any big rocks. I'm landing next time. You're right. We don't have any more time."

The last and final go round felt like it took an eternity. The risk of running out of gas could materialize any second. I kept waiting for the engine to cut out but cheered for it to make it. This was pushing our fate to the edge but we both believed that we would survive. Mike had the planes tires just inches from touching down. The wheels gently touched the ground and began to dig in. At first, we rolled straight and after about twenty yards the sand thickened.

We could feel the texture; soft, thick sand. We rolled on a short distance further and began to spin. The force of the spin threw our bodies together and we crashed into the sides of the plane. We traveled 180 degrees and tried to grab a piece of the plane for control. Suddenly, no movement.

I glanced out the window and saw golden particles of dust radiantly floating around the plane. The particles so thick, sparkled from the rays of sunlight and blinded us by their density. It was dark and light and dark again. Like a candle flickering against a soft breeze. We could not see more than a few inches. The dust cloud engulfed the entire plane. I worried the plane was on fire but Mike grabbed me and shouted, "We made it! Piece of cake. I guess we fish-tailed a little."

Mike began to say a short prayer of thanks. We were both saturated and exhausted by the ordeal. But we were alive.

YOU HAVE TO BE KIDDING ME!

We patiently waited for the dust cloud to settle back into the ground. My senses drew me to the fact that the plane was now facing the way we landed. We did more than just fish-tail; we did a complete 180 degree spin. The sand sucked us around and down; probably why we stopped so fast.

We both pondered how lucky we were when I couldn't wait any longer. I reached for the door and swung it open. Hot, dry, dirty air streamed into the plane. It coated our skin and burned our lungs. My eyes instantly watered and I wondered what we had gotten ourselves into. I pulled myself up and jumped down onto the wing of the plane. Two more steps and a jump and I would hit the ground and sink into the sand.

I was startled to see twelve eyes staring at me and watching my every move. Their hands were outstretched and their skinny bodies showed off their underdeveloped ribs. They were children, six to ten years old with their hands wide open and screaming for, "One American Dollar, Please."

I told Mike, "You're not going to believe this."

Mike's head had just peaked out of the door and a huge smile came across his face. "I guess they thought that was a pretty cool landing."

They had no clue to what we had just been through. It seemed they knew the routine. Planes land, they run out and get American dollars. It worked. I gave every kid a dollar and so did Mike. These children made out pretty well. They all ran away together, laughing, probably satisfied that they couldn't squeeze any more out of us. I saw no parents watching them or close by. I did take my first good look at the landscape and noticed that this was not an active airport. Some construction had started, small buildings mostly framed but none finished. Mike was walking around the plane checking for damage.

I noticed that at one time this was an orchard. They cut out a couple rows of trees and leveled a runway. The buildings were started but never finished and evidently abandoned. One red wind sock still remained daring the lost to land on a runway of dirt and sand.

I sarcastically said, "Well, this isn't LA-X."

Mike summed up his always optimistic thoughts, "Well it worked for us. However, I think we landed at the wrong place. This is not San Felipe airport. This is some place different. Can't be an airport! Can it?"

"Define airport!," I cracked, "Was the map outdated?"

"That's the latest map you could get. Something is very strange about this place."

I thought back to twenty five minutes earlier when I was looking through the binoculars at the landscape of San Felipe. I could see the ocean to the east with a four story hotel on the beach. Very little color seeped up from the ground; mostly brown and dirty red. Across from the hotel were single family homes that looked like a tent city. Lots of cardboard material and sheets; I could see very little wood. I saw some farms and groves of trees on a mostly flat earth. A main road divided the four star hotel from where the peasants lived; it was a dividing line of wealth and prestige. Our real destination was four hours away, La Paz. We had reservations at a four star hotel on the beach but it looked like we were going to be late.

"Mike, we have to make our way to the to the San Felipe Hotel and find out what's going on. We need some answers."

Mike stared at the plane stuck in the sand and said, "I think the plane's fine; no damage, not even to the tires. Amazing! We need to call ahead to La Paz. We might be a little late."

"You think." I jabbed.

We started to lock the plane down and felt comfortable it was safe; though it wasn't going anywhere. The wheels lodged half buried in the sand. The dust left clumps of dirt attached to the fuselage, the wings and tail were lathered in dust. Every inch of the plane looked awful. Mike's metaphysical child was a mess. I could tell he wanted to wash it; make it better. He kept walking around the plane with a glaze in his eyes and a lump in his throat. Was everything really okay?

Both our heads turned to look at what was coming toward us. It was still off in the distance, small but growing; spiraling up into the air in a circular motion building in intensity. Damn. It was another dust cloud. It moved toward us at a very rapid pace. No doubt, a car or truck was eager to get to us. It whipped toward our location weaving in and out of abandoned buildings. It almost fish-tailed around the last corner when we could finally see it; a truck. It slowed down and skidded in front of the plane. An old, graying man sprang from his seat. He grinned and showed off his tobacco stained teeth and I noticed he was missing a few. He spit a black stream of saliva to the ground that splattered all over our pants. He laughed out loud and said, "Bienvenidos. Necesitan gasolina?"

Was he for real? Maybe a ghost from the old airport? Mike never hesitated, "Hello. Fill her up!"

I bellowed, "You got to be kidding me. How do you know that he has jet fuel?"

"One, my planes not a jet. Two, we have little choice," Mike brought me back down. I said, "Look at this guy! Check out his pick-up. You're ready to risk our lives on what he has in the back of a pick-up?"

We walked over to the pick-up and then around it. I glanced at the inside and saw two cans of chewing tobacco on the cracked and torn seats. My eyes did a double take on the rack behind the seats that held two shotguns. That got my attention. The outside of the truck looked rusted scratched, and dented. No chrome, nothing polished, and no business name or sign. Three old drums sat in the back rusted and dirty. I saw an old siphoning hose with a metal connector at the end. The man just held out his hand toward the drums of gas; spat another spit of chew and smiled. I broke the silence, "Mike those drums could be filled with anything. Water, oil, dog shit. Do you really want to put that into your plane?"

"Yeah. We just lucked out. He's for real. It's time for us to have a little faith that God is watching us and is taking care of us. He got us through the landing, huh?" Have some faith. Filler up Jose," Mike ordered, "And check the water and oil!"

The man smirked and reached for the hose. It took forever to fill the plane and I watched Jose like a predator watching prey. All I could hear were Mike's words about having a little faith. Was this trip all about faith? I had been raised a Catholic; baptized days after birth. My mother would bring me to Mass Sunday after Sunday and we never missed a Holy Day. She signed me up to be an altar boy as soon as I qualified. It wasn't long before I was getting taller than the priests and Ruth, my mother, registered me to be a Reader. Eventually I became a Minister of Holy Communion. The greatest gift a mother can give her children is Faith. Of course, I learned that only God gives the graces of faith but he used my mother to get to me. He might have used my father in a completely different way. My mother and dad divorced when I was three. My mother remarried and really kept me away from my dad's side of the family. I would later find out that there were problems; abuse, addictions, alcoholism. Possibly murder on my dad's dad? The family seemed to manifest a self-destructive pathology. My father seemed to have the worst of these demons. He drank and smoked and had terrible ulcers eating away at his stomach. After many surgeries, his stomach ended up the size of a walnut. He was almost on a total liquid diet. When he committed suicide I was only 12. He was only 34.

He called me and said good-bye. I think I was the last person he talked to. He had everything to do with my faith. I was shocked and surprised but not devastated. I only saw him a few times a year. He helped coach my baseball and football teams but never really got close. I cried, mourned at the funeral and moved on. It would actually hurt me more later in life than it did when I was 12.

Shortly after the funeral I realized I had just lost my father. I needed a replacement. My step father wasn't the answer for me. In fact, he really never seemed to like me. The place I looked was God; the Father. The Trinity: Father, Son, and Holy Spirit, a theology that is covered in mystery; one God, three natures, all at the same time. Many theologians spend a lifetime trying to understand how this can happen but it was pretty simple to me. My faith became strong when I felt God the Father helping me through my life. Not only was this God my father, he had rules and regulations and traditions that were important.

It was a quick fix for me. I bought in and enjoyed everything that involved the church. I befriended, Father Kennedy, Father

Martin and now Father Mike Cross. I got to see them swear, get emotional, frustrated and even fail. I thought I was lucky to see them as human beings; flawed and damaged; just like me.

I met the Bishop and Mike's priestly circle of friends and always felt they were kind to me. I admired them. I found them to be good, intelligent people. You could tell the ones closest to God.

They had strong spirits. I especially liked the ones who could preach. They didn't all have this gift; that was obvious. I felt Mike had a strong spirit; and he was working on his preaching. He had more trust and faith in God's leading him than I did. It was something I would have to learn.

As it turned out I remembered enough Spanish to ask Jose his real name. Carlos. He didn't talk much but he did offer us a ride to the hotel. It was getting late in the afternoon so we needed to check in soon. Carlos drove like a crazy man to the hotel and spit tobacco into a little black cup on the dash. We thanked him and gave him a big tip and shut the door of his truck. He leaned over and said, "Dog shit!" and sped away laughing.

Carlos finally showed his true self. "Did you hear that?"

"I did, Mike smiled, Perfect English. How about that?"

"Mike he is either our guardian angel or our executioner. Did you see the shotguns in the back of his truck? Is God telling you he's a good man? He understood every word we said. He deceived us."

"No no no. He's a good man. He's just trying to survive. That fuel was good, I'm telling you. I tested it Nick. No more negativity. We're at a four star hotel on the beach in San Felipe. The water's supposed to be 80 degrees and the margarita's strong. Let's get some dinner. I'm starved." Mike pointed out the vacation part of our trip.

WE'RE DRUG RUNNERS?

We secured a room looking straight out at the ocean. We got a reservation for the late dinner sitting; we had missed the early one. I just wanted to get my bathing suit on and frolic in the water. Mike was right, some of the warmest water in the world was right at our doorstep.

Mike decided to stay in the room and make phone calls. He had to alert La Paz of our situation. I told him to find out about the San Felipe Airport. Where was it?

I started out slow but immediately felt warm sensations run up my leg. The water temperature was close to a comfortable hot tub; yet it was ocean water. Amazing! We were now close to the equator; a thermal blanket cast out onto the planet torching everything it touched. The water was incredibly soothing and calming. Relaxation followed. This was a nice present after this afternoon's events. The day was cooling down and the sunset was fast approaching. It would be spectacular. Everyone I could see enjoyed it! I hope Mike didn't miss it."

After I got back from my swim, I hustled up a shower and met up with Mike for dinner. He started, "You won't believe what I've discovered!"

"I interrupted, "Didn't you see the sunset?"

"I was working on our situation. I'm glad you enjoyed it." Mike said.

"Okay. What did you learn?" I questioned.

Mike rolled into everything he had learned, "That was an abandoned runway; an attempt at building an airport. The hotel wanted a closer airport; the one they got is nearly 45 minutes away. The project ran out of money and abandoned. Money was put into a shuttle service from the airport on the far north end of town. We somehow missed it!" By the way; it's a dirt field too."

I still had problems with the map. "Yes that all makes sense. What about the map? It has a printed landing strip right above an abandoned airport. People could use that map as a guide and go through what we just did."

"They have." Mike interrupted, "The drug smugglers! The project ended almost eight months ago. Since then lots of small planes have landed there. They only stay on the ground long enough to fill up and take off again."

"Carlos. He thought we were drug runners?" I surmised.

"Yes." Mike agreed.

"How did you get all this information? I questioned.

"The bartender." Mike exclaimed excited. "Carlos watches the sky and races to the planes for refueling. He makes a killing."

"I guess he wasn't impressed with our tip," I beat Mike to the joke.

"I know the fuel is okay so don't worry." Mike tried to ease my questions about the fuel.

"Mike, the children; did they think we were drug smugglers?" I was learning.

"Maybe," Mike jumped in, "What do kids know? However, I hope the federals leave us alone. I don't want to get involved with them. They can detain you for days. I have buddies who have told me."

"Mike, I left my marijuana at home. We don't have any contraband."

"You smoke marijuana?" Mike asked.

"A little." I couldn't lie. Besides; I kind of liked it.

"What's it like?" Mike was curious about everything; I didn't know this side of him.

"Mike, someday I will smoke some with you. Is there anything else I should know?"

Mike continued with what he learned, "Okay. Here's what I think. We have caused a slight buzz in the town. Everyone has treated me special.They think you and me are important people; maybe dangerous. They're trying to figure us out.

I think we should leave in the morning. We get up early and dig the plane out. La Paz awaits!" Mike's arms swung upward like he just scored a touchdown. I still had some questions:

"Dig out? Dig out. It might take days to get a long enough section clean for take-off; just getting the plane out of the sand could take an hour."

Mike quickly jumped in. "The whole second half of the runway is solid. The drug traffickers know to use the second half of the runway; the first is mostly a sand trap. We can do this."

"The bartender told you all this?" I jumped in.

Mike shook his head and smiled like some secret agent gathering information. I shot back, "That's incredible. I like the idea of people being a little scared of me. Maybe we should stay awhile and take advantage of our new found stature."

Mike added more information. "The bartender says the federales will be here within 48 hours. We need to be gone by tomorrow."

"Okay, but we both agree the conditions are safe for take-off.

If I don't like what I see we don't take off, okay?" I stared at Mike.

"Okay. Of course! You're my co-pilot." Mike patted my back as he spoke. I immediately wanted to talk to the bartender. I asked Mike to lead me straight away to the man who told Mike about the airfield. We landed in a sand trap.

Without some luck and skill we should have nosedived into the sand; dead. I wanted to know the real condition of the runway. Mike pointed him out. He was much younger than I expected, a clean shaven, handsome man. He motioned that he saw us and headed right to our end of the bar. Before he could say a word I belted out, "Okay, how long is the sand?"

I guess I could have introduced myself, however, I had things on my mind. Plus, I thought I was a bad dude. This guy was scared of me, or so I perceived.

"The first half, all sand. Start at the end of the sand; hard ground the rest of the way; all the way to the end. Planes do it every day. Just start your take-off at the half way mark." The bartender told me exactly what I wanted to know. Clever.

"Well, okay then," I turned to Mike, "Do you want a margarita?"

"No. I don't drink on the night before I fly. And we are flying in the morning!", Mike said forcefully.

"Is it ok for passengers to drink? I raised my eyebrows for permission.

"No problem, Nick" Mike turned to the bartender and said, "One margarita and one without alcohol, please."

"You mean a virgin?" The bartender belted out smiling.

I had to jump in, "Yes, that will do." I laughed and hit Mike in the stomach.

I stared right at and asked the only question that mattered, "Can you get the plane up with only half a runway?"

"I think so. I didn't really measure how long we have. That job will be important in the morning." Mike didn't seem confident. He glanced at me and said, "You're my co-pilot. We don't fly unless you are comfortable with the conditions." Mike patted my back as he finished.

How would I know if the conditions were unsafe? How many feet did the Archer need to get airborne? It had to take longer on a dirt field, there was no pavement in sight. So many variables crossed my mind; how could I know if it was safe? For me, I guess it would just have to be a gut feeling. My gut wasn't feeling so good. This was going to be Mikes call; only a real pilot could understand what we were up against. It was obvious: it was time to get out town.

WHAT A LIFE

We rose early and preceded directly to the plane. Our plane was stuck in the middle of trouble. It made sense, a refueling depot for drug smugglers. We had to get out of here as rapidly as we could. I was relieved when I saw the plane.

When we reached the runway the hot sun was ready to deliver its morning jolt. How could it be so hot so early? I sweated from just thinking about digging. The Piper 180 was buried half up to its wheels, stuck. It would require some effort to dislodge the plane. After fifteen minutes I was drenched and sucking in air. Mike stopped me and evaluated our predicament. "That's enough! We can use the plane's engines to supply enough inertia to get the plane free."

"Are you sure? I'm happy to stop digging." I whimpered.

"Yeah. We just have to point the plane in the right direction. We have to start it almost at the end of the sand. Nick, check the ground all the way to the end. Make sure it's solid and no rocks!"

I walked and surveyed the entire second half of the runway. I poked the ground every five feet to feel its texture. It felt hard and smooth. Planes, lots of them had literally polished the ground in front of me. Once again I felt confident that the plane could reach take-off velocity. I ran back to the plane feeling pretty good. My new anxieties revolved around the gas. Was it real? I felt it was time for me to step forward and make a leap of faith.

We could make this work. God was protecting us; at least it felt that way. I yelled at Mike, "Okay. Let's make this happen!"

Mike stared off into the distance in a stoic poise; arms crossed, petrified in thought.

"We have a problem."

"What are you talking about?" I jumped in.

Look at the far end of the runway," Mike pointed to the problem, "It's a telephone wire or electrical wire. Why put a telephone wire at the end of a runway? We need to clear that. The drug runners make it; so it's doable."

I stared at the wire; jaw half open. How did I miss that? I guess I was looking at the dirt on the runway, I had never bothered to look up, but there it was.

"Doable?" Are you sure?" I wanted some assurance.

"Yeah! Though it's going to be one short take-off," a nervous pilot lectured.

"Oh my God!" Pause. "That isn't using the Lord's name in vain is it, Mike?"

"No no no. I use that saying all the time. It's intent, mixed with emotion and disrespect that insults the name of God." Mike preached.

"I like that." I continued, "Emotion: disrespect. Yeah, I'm just scared. Is the vacation over?"

Mike stated what he had maintained all along. "Hey, we are on an adventure, I can get the plane over that wire. Not a problem"

Mike's ability to manifest faith was remarkable. He really thought that God had put that obstacle in our path and would help us get over it. I started shaking my head and bantered, "Can't we have a little break in all the drama?"

"What a life! We'll never forget this place or this trip. I promise you." Mike predicted.

We both climbed into the plane and readied it for take-off. I was getting better at my pre flight responsibilities. I enjoyed being the co-pilot and knew Mike would let me fly the plane as some point on the trip; but not now. Mike positioned the plane at the mid-point of the runway. He revved up the engine to check for take-off power. He seemed happy about the performance of the plane. My mind crept back to Carlos and rusty barrels of gas. I would know soon what was really in those cans. All my earlier faith evaporated when Mike pointed out the telephone wire across the end of the runway. It would be over fast, one way or another. Mike's optimism and faith stood strong; amazing. We needed speed and a quick take-off. Mike looked at me and we both blessed ourselves and he released the brakes. The wheels rolled smoothly and we picked up speed. My eyes were fixated to the far end of the runway, and the wire we needed to clear. I perceived the obstacle getting closer and closer and we were still on the ground. It seemed impossible to clear it and my stress level was again off the charts. Finally, we lifted off the ground. Slowly, methodically, we rose. The wire was right on top of us when I screamed, "Pull back!"

Mike pulled the control stick back with strength and control. The plane's propeller cleared the wire but the new concern was the wheels hanging below the fuselage. They could catch and drag us straight down. It was over in a second. In unison, we both bellowed out a scream in high "C". We made it.

"Just a little faith." I said, suddenly feeling brave, perhaps even cocky. What was happening to me? This adventure was starting to change me.

"What a life!" Mike said with relieve resonating from his voice. My shirt was completely wet; saturated again by my over active armpits and it was barely past 8am. Onward to La Paz.

NICO

Mike climbed to 5,500 feet leveled out and began cruising. We were going 125mph with clear visibility and a full tank of gas. He always reminded me that the most dangerous part of flying were the take-offs and landings. Reaching cruising altitudes was the safest. How smooth the ride was: was a whole different matter. Unequal heating of the ground affected the air currents and wind speed. Air currents, like ocean waves raising and crashing would treat the plane like a boat adrift. In modern jets you barely felt the ripples. In a Piper 180 you felt everything.

My stomach floated between my throat and belt line and bounced like a ball. I would get air sick from the extremes. Still, I was getting used to the sensations and tried to anticipate them and relax. My breathing was also involved in staying calm. At the moment, we were in a nice calm bubble of air. I was exhausted. REM sleep evaded me the last 48 hours. Too much excitement: too much to think about. Suddenly, the plane quickly dropped into another hard pocket of air which startled us both. "Just a little bump." Mike calmly stated.

"I hate those." I said.

"It's the unequal heating of the ground. It creates pockets of unstable air."

"I know. Move the plane up. It's smoother up there." I pointed up.

24

Mike moved the plane up to 7,500 feet and found some solitude from the turbulence. The plane reacted to Mike much better in this air. Mike had a smile on his face and gave me a thumbs up. He predicted, "Nothing but smooth sailing for you Nico!"

"Nico?" I have not been called that since my high school Spanish class. "Gracias Miguel." I cracked back.

My name is Nicholas Howard Adams and I was born in Santa Cruz, California. It didn't bother me being called Nico, it sounded rough and important. I was already labeled a drug runner in San Felipe; so the name fit. I had a girlfriend back in California who I would one day marry. We met at San Jose State; working on our teaching credentials.

I knew I wanted to be a teacher since my sophomore year in high school. However, my real passion was coaching. I played sports from the time I could run and throw a ball. I was an athlete; coordinated and lean. I joined junior leagues in all sports and signed up for the swim team. I had success at all levels but I always admired my coaches. They provided the necessary knowledge of the movements and skill in managing a game. I watched them and learned what seemed to work and what didn't. I also followed all the professional athletes. I would memorize the player statistics for all the sports but especially baseball. I yearned to be a professional baseball player; a goal of thousands of young boys. I had some success and played baseball into college. I was invited to a free agent tryout with the Oakland A's. That was the day my dream ended. However, it pushed me in a new direction; coaching.

At that time, you had to have a teaching job to coach a high school sport. The first goal would be to get a teaching credential. I had shared my plans with Mike, who supported me. Needless to say, I realized that part of our friendship from his point of view, was to make me a priest. I certainly had the qualifications and the love of the church. God the Father, circulated those thoughts in my head. I needed a vocation; it was a possibility. I also felt a strong calling to raise a family and do it right; no divorce. I imagined my dichotomy would unfold on its own terms and pull me one way or another. I knew what Mike was rooting for. I had barely thought about my girlfriend since we left. I now had three hours to get ready for a La Paz landing. I proceeded to get into my sentinel watch mode. I could not sleep while we were in the air so I positioned my eyes on the horizon. I surveyed every inch we flew over and checked in on Mike to keep him alert. I didn't know we were just hours away from our next big problem.

JET-WASH

We flew on a calm pocket of air for almost an hour. I surrendered to a sleep deprived state when Mike brought me back. "Hey. We're making good time. Should be there soon. La Paz is an international airport with paved runways. It can safely land even the biggest jets. No more drama, Nico."

"Sounds great." I responded. Since I was a little kid I loved watching the giant jet airplanes. They fascinated me, nearly hypnotizing my senses. I couldn't believe how the 747 jet could get off the ground. They seemed to break the laws of physics. I would stare for hours at the take-offs and landings. It all looked like a miracle to me "I can't wait to see those big jets from the tarmac." I was excited.

"We don't want to get too close." Mike reasoned. "We'll probably land in another section of runway away from the jets. The jet's engines create a wake turbulence of very unstable air behind it. This backwash is nasty and unpredictable. We could lose control of the plane."

I jumped back in, "How do we know where to land?"

"The terminal. It's time to make contact."

Mike worked the radio to the frequency for La Paz airport and we made contact. We were both surprised to find out we were being placed in a landing rotation right behind a 737 jet. Doubling our trouble, we also found out we were landing on the

27

same runway as the big jet. Mike shook his head and motioned to me that we would fall back, putting distance between us and the jet. I turned; a small plane came into view behind us. We were squeezed in the middle. It was perilous. We both felt uncomfortable.

"Mike we can't fall back; there is a plane behind us. Are we going to be okay?" I questioned.

"Oh yeah, I'm sure they will space us out. It could get a little bumpy." Mike gasped for air.

"Can't we have a simple landing?" I shouted.

"Not on this adventure." Mike shot back. "God is with us. We need to catch his energy. Just a little faith and trust, Mike preached. "Faith and trust."

Relational theology says we are all connected to God. A cosmic stream of energy that flows inside each of us. Mike believed it. His faith was strong enough to feel God's presence. He had a relationship. Let God lead. What would Jesus Do? All slogans that sounded nice but required enormous leaps of faith. I thought I had faith but it was being tested. Again I took a deep breath and showed as much courage as I could muster. Stay calm; avoid becoming hysterical. I glanced at the jet as it started descending and could hear it's engines starting to reverse. Everything seemed normal; however, a huge invisible shock wave of air was being created and we were heading right for it. We were only 100 feet off the ground on final approach when the wave hit us.

"Hang on, we're caught in its wake turbulence." Mike gasped as the plane immediately dropped and pulled to the left. "I can't fight it. It's like a rip tide of air."

"Pull up! Pull up!" I shouted.

The turbulence tossed us left across the cockpit; Mike hit his head against the door and I crashed into Mike. Our bodies popped up and down and I could feel the seat belt jam into my stomach. For a second, Mike had lost control of the plane.

"Jet wash" He said while shaking his head. "Hang on."

Mike banked left hard to get away from the unstable air. The plane responded and climbed hard. It took a few seconds but Mike gained total control. We circled back behind the last plane in the lineup and alerted the terminal. Mike asked to be inserted behind a smaller plane. Permission was granted. The voice over the radio held some concern, "Are you guys okay?"

Mike acknowledged our safety and reminded the terminal of the wake turbulence problems we encountered. The air traffic controller's statement was, "You guys were lucky."

Beads of sweat lined up on Mike's forehead; his face twisted with stress. His first concern, as always, was me. "You okay? That was a little rough."

"Was the plane out of control?" I knew the answer but I had to ask the question.

"Maybe for a second. Just can't fight that air. That's the worst jet wash I've ever flown through." Mike reminisced.

"You've been through that before?" I asked.

"Oh yeah. Many times. Never like that." Mike started laughing and apologized for the ordeal. He promised a perfect landing.

I was completely shaken but after a perfectly greased landing my eyes surveyed the large jets that were all around us. I instantly calmed down. Going into a child-like state, I gazed at the size of the planes we were taxing towards. I relaxed and enjoyed La Paz's airport tarmac. People come here from all over the world. However, without my consent, a deep, dark thought crept into my subconscious. It had nothing to do with airports or airplanes. This was a thought dripping with despair and demise. How could I possibly make it all the way back home alive? We had come a long way and survived a couple of rough landings. A celestial stream of good fortune seemed to descended on us. I needed to tap into that stream and create some positive energy of my own. I didn't like going to my dark place. I needed more faith, more courage.

The plane stopped. I instantly opened the door. It was hotter than San Felipe. The jets around us hissed with noise and power. I yelled to Mike, "I need a margarita!"

"Me too!" Mike agreed.

LA PAZ

The La Paz hotel, the hotel Sol/Mar was modest, quaint and ordinary. Two blocks from the beach; it had a rustic historical gleam to it. It was not a resort, more like a bed and breakfast. Our room was small, with two single beds, a living room and bathroom with shower. The hotel's restaurant was well decorated and clean. I saw some Americans eating when we walked in and figured the place must be legitimate. It also served complimentary breakfast. The real, four star, resorts were right on the beach next to the Harbor. The Harbor supported all kinds of fishing boats in all shapes and sizes. The water was courtesy of the Sea of Cortez; which held seafood treasures so abundant, fishermen came from all over the world to test their skills. Giant swordfish, mahi, mahi, or dolphin were plentiful and on every menu. You could see anything from sharks to stingrays, giant sea turtles to coral reefs. Tomorrow, we had a fishing excursion hopefully to battle a swordfish and go snorkeling in the crystal clear water of the Sea of Cortez.

We quickly unpacked and stretched out on our beds. We both needed some relaxation; some decompression time. I was ready for a long nap when Mike said, "What a life."

"Well, somehow we're still alive," I responded, "Yeah that's good. I'm excited about the fishing and snorkeling tomorrow. Do you think we'll see a swordfish?"

I hope so, Nico." Mike continued to speak. "You know, we don't really know how to fish We just go trolling and when we catch a fish; jump into a chair and hold on for dear life."

"I hear it could take 45 minutes to get a swordfish to the boat." I pretended I knew something about fishing.

"Could be longer. Anyhow the snorkeling is said to be spectacular. I'm bushed and ready for my siesta." Mike fell quiet.

Exhausted we both melted into an afternoon slumber. I only slept for about 45 minutes when Mike's constant, loud snoring woke me up solidly. A light sleeper, I needed silence to enjoy sleep. No matter, I popped up, grabbed my guitar and headed for the Harbor. The setting sun would be perfect motivation to play. The walk felt short and I found a park bench looking straight out at the Harbor. Trained in classic rock I tuned my guitar and started strumming away. A local man walked up to my position and sat nervously close to me. The man was lightly bearded, with dark skin and a mustache. He sat on a rock adjacent to my spot. He spoke a short greeting in Spanish and rocked his head back and forth, manifesting his enjoyment of the music. I played on, enjoying my new audience of one. The sun began to set on the horizon directly in front of us. A palm tree acted like a canopy above us and swayed by a soft breeze. The silhouettes of the boats in the harbor reflected on the blue water. Amazingly, the local man was still sitting, legs folded, beside me. I'm sure almost an hour had gone by. He smiled and bobbed his head to the time of the music. He would clap after I was done.

My fingers were getting sore as the last rays of sunlight extinguished on the horizon. I had to get back for dinner. What a connection I had with this local man; we both smiled and shook hands as we parted. I glanced behind me and saw Mike taking some pictures with his camera.

"Did you get a picture of me and that guy?"

"Yep. Looks like you found a friend." Mike smiled and continued, "Was it my snoring?"

"You were loud. I'm a light sleeper." I let out.

"How long was that guy listening to you?" Mike questioned.

"He sat there for an hour, didn't say two words. Just smiled and moved his head to the beat of the song." I exclaimed, dumbfounded.

"Music bridges languages, cultures, any obstacle really." Mike profoundly stated.

"I guess so. I was playing rock and roll; the Doobie Brothers! He would have never heard any of their work."

"Who are the Doobie Brothers?" Mike questioned.

"Are you kidding me old man? The Doobie Brothers rock!"

"I guess he liked it. Did you try 'La bamba'?" Mike joked.

"I played everything I knew. I won't forget that guy; what a memory." I joyful exclaimed.

We hustled back to the Hotel Sol/Mar to get ready for dinner. Our fishing excursion started at the crack of dawn so we agreed to an early evening. However, the evening turned out to be anything but early.

MONTEZUMA'S REVENGE

We both confronted the drinking water problems aggressively, especially Mike. He brought pills to disinfect the micro bugs that were in the water in Baja California. From day one, he lectured on avoiding Montezuma's Revenge: a sickness from the microbes in the drinking water. The symptoms were diarrhea and nausea. You could have both symptoms at the same time. Not a pleasant image. I would only drink bottled water and beer. Mike popped his pills, even into bottled water, "I am sure all the local hotels have good water," Mike reminded me. "But we can't be too careful."

"So far so good" I smiled. "Let's get two special margaritas to celebrate our good fortune so far."

"Sounds good," Mike perked up.

We enjoyed a tasty delight of mahi for dinner. Giving in to temptation, we downed two more margarita's and I topped it off with a shot of Grand Marnier. The alcohol snuck up on both of us. However, I tolerated the effect much better than Mike. I thought back to my fraternity parties at San Jose State, just a few months earlier. Kegs of free beer, music, and girls all between 10th and 11th streets. The fraternities looking for recruits rolled out the red carpets. We always pretended to be interested but never joined. This alcoholic frenzy of partying more than trained me for life. I could drink Mike under the table which is exactly what was happening. Mike's body was slumping down, his eyes almost level to the table. His face flushed, body wobbled, and eyes glazed over. "Mike you okay?"

"Yes sir. The alcohol has gone straight to my head." Mike tried to stand but had to grab the table for support. The table shifted from the weight and all the glasses danced nearly falling over.

"Hey, you okay?" I questioned again.

"Yes sir. I'm afraid I am a bit drunk. Could you get me back to the shroom?"

"No problem. You landed a plane on dirt field, I'll get you to your shroom?" I laughed.

I carted Mike out of the restaurant; one arm under his shoulder and another around his back.

I didn't want to draw any attention but I could sense people watching us. I could feel the weight of Mike trying to hold him up. He walked slowly and kept saying how sorry he was. I got him up to the room and dropped him on his bed.

"I'm so sorry. I usually don't drink that much. Don't like to drink anything when I'm flying. Glad we're not flying tomorrow." Mike's tired eyes started to close as he spoke.

"We're fishing tomorrow," I reminded him.

"Thanks for the help. Let's keep this to ourselves. I wouldn't want this to get around the parish, you know. I'm not an old drunk." Mike was embarrassed.

"No worries. We're on vacation." I said finally feeling like I was on a vacation.

Mike quickly succumbed to an alcohol induced sleep and I followed right behind him. I had to fall asleep before he starting snoring or it would be a long night. Though I was tired sleep eluded me and my stomach ached from gas pains. I let out flatulence to get some comfort but it came right back. It was going to be a long night. The insomnia from the pain finally drove me into the bathroom. The diarrhea though unwelcome, brought me some relieve. My thoughts raced to Mike's lecture on Montezuma's Revenge. How could this be? A small panic attack of anxiety flooded my body. Was this sickness from the food or the water? My brain frantically searched for the reason for my misery.

"You okay?" Mike yelled from just the other side of the bathroom door.

"Don't know?" I'm sick, diarrhea. Mike is this Montezuma's Revenge?"

"No. No. No. We never drank anything but bottled water," Mike stated. "You just have a little upset stomach."

"How do you feel Mike? Do you feel sick?"

"I feel fine. I do have a slight headache but otherwise just fine."

Mike and I started to name everything we ate and drank. The first clue came from Mike. "We both had salads; right?"

"Yeah." I said sitting on the pot.

"They wash the lettuce with water. Hey that could be it," Mike concluded.

"You're not sick. What about the Margaritas? Ice comes from local water sources. Oh my God, "I've got Montezuma's Revenge," I panicked.

"Calm down," Mike bellowed looking around the door to see if I was alright. "It's possible but I'm not sick. Plus this hotel caters to Americans. No, it's as simple as a little indigestion to the local cuisine."

The rest of the night I made a path from my bed to the bathroom. I don't know how many trips I made before it finally calmed down. I slept more on the toilet than the bed that night. I couldn't get comfortable. I also couldn't go out on a fishing boat like this. I could not fly like this either. At least, I wasn't puking. I wondered what could possibly happen next.

LET'S GO FISHING

Mike sprang up initiating his morning routine. Everyday, so far, he got up thirty minutes before me; sometimes an hour. He would go straight to the bathroom and shut the door. It was strange for me but didn't concern me; none of my business. Besides, since he was like clockwork every morning; I knew I had one hour of sleep left. My deepest sleep seemed to initiate during this period. My stomach settled down enough for me to sleep. I needed to recharge some energy. Finally, I was feeling comfortable enough to make these sixty minutes count.

"Hey Nico! How do you feel?" Mike came out of nowhere.

"Don't you need more time?" I pleaded not believing sixty minutes were up.

"We can't miss the boat." Mike reminded me. "Do you feel well enough to do this? We can cancel the excursion. You won't enjoy it if you're sick."

I could see the concern in his whole body. "Let's go fishing," I said, springing out of bed. I would not let Mike down. He wanted to fish badly so running on fumes, I could gut this out. After breakfast, mostly fluids and scrambled eggs, I noticed a burst of energy that made me feel much better. We hustled down to the Harbor and proceeded to board our boat. It was big; over forty-five feet, with a huge elevated cabin and two chairs in the back that looked like something you would see in a barber shop. It also had a bathroom. I studied the chairs in the back. They almost reminded me of a lazy-boy recliner. Soft padded arm rests and a soft seat tempted you to sit. However, I realized that no one sat there until we had a fish. I could see the seat belts and shoulder straps; these chairs meant you were going to be on the fight of your life. I couldn't wait.

Two local fishermen and a captain made up the crew. I was shocked to learn we were the only two passengers. The ship could hold many more but with just two of us it would double our odds of catching a fish. Plus, we would corner all the attention and hospitality of the crew. The captain, speaking in Spanish, lashed out with confidence and authority. He motioned for us to sit down and relax. "We have a case of beer, a nice lunch, and we will catch a Marlin for you today. My crew will teach you how to use the chairs, however, do not sit in them until we get a catch. Have a great time. I will be running The ship from above." He pointed to the control booth, just above the deck. Perfect English, I was impressed!

A soft breeze created by our momentum leaving the harbor felt soothing; a welcome gift to my tired body. I could see other boats initiate departure procedures. In all, I counted five boats getting underway. It was fast and furious. Who could get out first? This created a bottleneck at the mouth of the Harbor. Our captain waved to the closest boat to lead us out. You could tell they all knew each other and had engaged in this race before. I could see other crews on boats laughing and waving their arms. I'm sure they had side bets on who would catch the first Marlin. That's what this was all about, and the big tip they would get if their boat did capture their elusive prey. Every day, fishing in the Sea of Cortez; heaven on Earth for them.

We cruised fast, always within sight of the other boats. The crew was busy getting the fishing rods ready. I watched them cutting bait and securing the fishing lines. I turned back to the cabin and gazed upon the ice chest filled with the case of beer. I motioned to Mike to check it out, "That's all for us?"

Mike came back, "Probably for the crew too."

"I see some bottled water, are they okay to drink?" I asked.

Absolutely," Mike pulled his pills out his pocket.

"Ok what do we do now?" I wondered.

"Sit back and enjoy the ride. I can't wait to sit in those chairs and fight a big fish." Mike pointed to the two empty chairs; waiting for action. "What a life Nico. What a life."

Mike placed his hands behind his head and stretched out on the bench we were allowed to sit on while we waited. The bench was long, cushioned, and comfortable. Adding to the mix was a light spray of water churning up from the front of the boat. The water hit my face and kept me exhilarated and fresh. The ride was beautiful but, little by little I noticed we were becoming separated from all the other boats. In just a short time I realized that we would be on our own. The crew got the poles ready: it was time to start trolling; slowly, at first, then with urgency. The Captain's discretion was to vary our speeds and angles. He never went straight; he constantly talked to the other boats on the radio and I wondered how many years he had performed this act. He was intense. Nothing to do but watch and admire. I was feeling better, Montezema's revenge had not manifest itself; I was relieved. I popped open my first beer before 11. The captain; talking on the radio to another boat signaled excitedly to his crew. His arm made a quick circle above his head which was the sign to get our lines out of the water. I asked one of the crew what was going on. He said in broken English, "Boat caught Marlin. We move. New place. Fishing better."

"Another boat caught a Marlin? I'll be damned." Mike joined in.

It was only fifteen minutes later that our lines were back in the water. We were trolling again. I could see two other boats in the area. These fishermen were connected by the thrill of success and their radios. They worked together and obviously had fun doing it. Seconds later it happened.

A crew member grabbed my pole and motioned for me to get in the seat and buckle up. Finally a bite; something was still on the line. He worked the pole around his body and got ready to hand it to me. I was nervously still trying to buckle myself in the chair. Mike reached around and helped me finish the job.

The excitement level on the ship rose when we realized we had another bite on the opposite pole. Mike jumped in his seat and prepared himself; reaching for the pole. I was handed my pole and locked the end into a metal hole down by my feet. Mike did the same. What were the odds of getting bites on both lines at the same time?

I reeled and pulled hard; this wasn't a little trout. This fish was strong. I could feel its size and power. Hopefully it was a marlin. I pulled harder; too hard evidently. A crew member chastised me and told me to ease up. Too early to put so much strain on the line.

Mike was equally enthralled. Everyone waited for the fish to jump; a trademark show for a marlin. Only minutes into the struggle found our lines crossing and a giant tangle unfolding.

Suddenly, out of nowhere, the captain leaped from behind Mike and cut his line. He motioned to the crew to put their energy into my fish.

"Sorry bro. We could have lost both fish; the lines were

getting tangled. This way we still have one." He smiled and jetted back up to his perch above us.

Mike, stunned by the suddenness of the captain's move, quickly recovered and supported me. I felt disappointment for Mike but I was too busy to do anything about it. Five minutes passed when the fish, huge by my untrained eye, jumped out of the water giving away his identity.

I saw no sword; no marlin. I wasn't let down, though I heard Mike say, "It's not a marlin. It's a mahi. Still the biggest fish you ever battled."

"You can say that again; still very strong." I spit out while reeling and pulling. Without the restraints I would have been launched out of my chair. Amazing!

Twenty minutes marked the time my arms began to cramp. I don't know how much more of this I could take. Still, everyone pushed me on. I didn't want to let anyone down and I was finally able to get the fish just behind the boat. To me, it was a monster. The crew nearly had it secure when a huge splash of water erupted from the back of the ship, my fish seamed stunned and stopped moving entirely.

The crew jumped back and yelled, "Shark. Shark! Shark!"

"What do you mean shark?" I didn't see a shark." I couldn't see over the back of the boat.

The captain screamed at the crew and they grabbed a long hook and paddles and started hitting the water. My fish totally stopped moving. The captain joined in and together they quickly pulled my fish into our boat. Silence. Then the crew and Captain, erupted into laughter. Mike just shook his head. I was trying to unbuckle the straps so I could see the giant mahi. I couldn't believe what I saw. My beautiful, forty or fifty pound mahi had a huge hole in his side. My jaw slowly opened as I saw the blood dripping from the giant bite mark.

"Plenty still to eat, Nick," Mike tried to downplay the event. "I never saw the shark. Did you?" I questioned.

"Honestly, no." Mike said, "But the evidence is irrefutable. Yep, a shark bit your fish. They saw it."

The captain said he had seen this before. He told us a couple of stories but pointed out that you usually lose the whole fish. He said I was lucky to get so much of it into the boat. The captain motioned to the crew to get the poles ready again and we proceeded to troll for another hour. Mike's catch came just as the captain was signaling to start getting the lines out of the water.

Mike sprang up and bolted for his chair. He harnessed himself in so fast he didn't need my help. One of the workers handed Mike his pole and he readied himself for a fight. "What a life, Nico. Can you believe this? Mike shouted.

I was still stunned from my experience with my Mahi. I shot back to Mike, "I will watch for the jump. I'll try to identify it!"

I watched Mike enjoy every second of time; totally in the moment. He almost professionally wrestled another mahi to the boat in 20 minutes. The crew easily recovered the fish; no bite marks and maybe bigger than mine.

Mike was speechless, exhausted. He glanced up at me and gave me a high five. "Can you believe that?" he excitedly questioned.

"Great job Mike. That was awesome. It will be interesting to see which fish is bigger. Of course, we will have to add a few pounds to mine. I'm just saying", I professed.

Mike shot back, "Let's call it a tie!" A priest's wisdom.

I agreed. It was inspiring to watch someone enjoy their life so completely. Fearlessly. No boundaries. Still, I knew he had the rules and regulations of the church, after all, he was a

Catholic priest. Mike seemed to be letting his guard down. The stress of many years of parish work had eased and father Cross was acting like an eighteen year old adolescent. He reached for a beer and delighted in his accomplishment. We both did.

I popped open another beer and toasted Mike and said, "Let's go snorkeling!"

Mike agreed, and we headed back to the shallower water. The Captain would certainly know the hottest snorkeling spot. The Sea of Cortez was his baby. These waters held some of the best snorkeling in the world. The clear water revealed a living museum of life.

The Captain said to relax; lunch would be served and we would slowly move toward a snorkeling spot he hoped we would enjoy. He sat quite close to us and told us that we would be in water that held great treasures of coral and fish. However, he warned us we would be in 30 feet of water. He stressed he and his crew would be watching everything around us. Predators lurk in the water too!" He grinned but it wasn't funny.

I glanced at Mike; eyes wide open. "Predators?"

Mike looked at me and saluted with his beer, "No worries, Nico!"

My mind was racing to all the predators when I bellowed out, "Sea snakes!"

Mike followed, "Well that's one. You would be dead in minutes from that one. I was thinking about another one. Teeth, hungry, big! What happened to your mahi?"

My mind went blank. Suddenly, the memory crashed through my thoughts. I shouted out, "Sharks!"

Mike shook his head. "I can't decide what would be worst, sea snake or shark. Of course we can't forget electric eels, snapping turtles and stinging jelly fish."

My only response was "Oh" and I fell quiet.

Mike smiled and told me not to worry and belted out laughing. He pointed out that the water would be clear, with great visibility. The boat would be close by and we couldn't let anything spoil this moment. This was going to be the greatest snorkeling experience of our lives. That was a lot to ask for. We weren't disappointed.

WAS THAT A MANTA RAY?

My arms ached from the workout with the mahi, but I still managed to enjoy lunch and a cold beer. The captain educated me on the history of my catch. My fish actually had three names; mahi, dorado, and dolphin fish. The locals latched on to dorado; not wanting to have people think they were hunting dolphins; although the dorado was part of the dolphin family.

He told me the Hotel would pay to have it cleaned and filleted. Heck, they would even put the fish into container filled with dry ice. It gave me the opportunity to bring the catch home. It would be a meal I would share with all my friends and family if I made it home alive.

I couldn't help but become cynical. I had survived two landings, a harrowing take-off, Montezuma's Revenge and a shark attack upon my prize dorado. I had every right to be cynical but confidence and courage slowly crept back into my thoughts. I was surprised to feel so cocky but I enjoyed these feelings of success.

The captain slowed the boat motioning to get ready to snorkel. Our captain had to know the most awesome snorkeling spot in the whole Sea of Cortez. Reefs, coral beds, manta rays, giant sea turtles and all sorts of colorful fish would come to life just below us.

The Captain spoke looking directly at us, "We will look out

for sharks. You look for rays and turtles. Do not go too far from the boat; you might have to get back quickly."

"I guess that means sharks, Nick. Stay on high alert." Mike cautioned

"No kidding. He just took all the fun out of it." I jumped into the water and immediately glared both directions for any predators. However, my eyes almost melted when the color from the reef and fish flashed across my field of vision.

Mike followed me in and we swam together for about 15 yards. I didn't want to get too far from the boat but right below us was an incredible coral reef with hundreds of fish of all shapes and colors. Keeping our life vest on made us buoyant, we didn't have to work to stay afloat. Just look down and enjoy.

Mike hit the top of my head, forcing me to look almost sideways; it was worth it. A huge Sea Turtle swam directly below us. Needless to say, for my money, the best location on the planet to snorkel. All the hype and reputation of this place came to fruition. The captain gave us one full hour before he wanted us back. The time seemed to evaporate in minutes and before we knew it the captain was yelling and waving for us to get back to the boat.

We both begged for five more minutes, and he granted our request. My mask hit the water quickly, crashing back to the giant school of fish. We had seen so much; but not the rays. We really wanted five more minutes to find a manta ray. This time I saw it first. I grabbed Mike's head and pivoted his neck to see the giant Ray that was swimming into view. Its size got our attention; it glided, effortlessly below. The wings separated majestically as in flight.

It enormous size made me feel uneasy, small, yet another followed close behind. Incredible. Two minutes of entertainment for our eyes; what a show. The second Ray sailed out of our sight and ended our discovery. It was time to get back to the ship. We talked as we swam toward the back of the ship. "Did you see those rays?" Mike shouted.

"Yes, I showed them to you; remember? Wow, that was way cool." I sounded like a teenager.

"Never seen any Ray that big; the first one, probably female, huge. The second male, smaller but not by much; a pair. Do you think love is in the air?" Mike gasped as he worked his way up the ladder.

"I thought the same thing. Mating. Hey how do you know the big one was the female? Listen to us; we're talking like experts. We don't know anything about the mating rituals of Manta Rays." I pulled myself up out of the water and unto the boat.

It didn't take long to connect all the empty beer cans to a party! I wondered how they could drink so much in just one hour but the fiesta had definitely broken out. The Captain and Crew were singing and laughing but still helping us out of the water. Mike laughed and whispered to me "Nick; they are all drunk."

The captain spoke making Mike's point, "Someone had to drink the beer. We saved you two!" Everyone laughed.

We both reached for the beers, the captain staggered up to his controls, started the vessel and we headed back to the Harbor. "Mike, what does your faith have to say about this situation?"

"Nico, smooth sailing ahead. No worries. No problems. God has given this man the gift to get us home; sober or drunk. You know they do this every day. They are just having fun; hell he's probably on top of his game after a few belts.

"A few belts? They almost drank the whole case", I pointed out.

"God will get us all the way back to eat that dorado with your family. What a story. A shark bite; incredible snorkeling; drunk guides; what more do you want?" Mike pulled more discernment out of his ocean of faith.

I had been lucky. The priests that I had a chance to have a friendship with seemed to possess personality traits that made it easy for them to enjoy life. They didn't seem to hold anything back; no fear. I admired them. People who could let go: take life on its own terms. You had to take some risk to get anything out of life; I was slowly being pulled in that direction. However, I wasn't ready to totally let go. I wanted to call some of the shots. Egocentric thoughts hold on tight to old habits. Every experience we shared made me think more about my faith. I looked at Mike's body language. He was thrilled at everything that had happened so far. Mike's faith manifested these strengths.

I shivered from the cool air hitting my wet body. It felt great. The day was still hot, well over ninety degrees. I huddled next to Mike holding my beer. I saluted him and offered up a toast.

"Mike, may all of our landings be happy landings."

Mike countered, "They say that any landing that you walk away from is a happy landing!"

"I'll drink to that!" I gulped down a large swallow of beer.

"Boy does beer taste good after what we've experienced today." Mike had a beer mustache as he spoke.

Mike's faith manifested strongly again. He had a connection; a relationship with God. Mike wasn't scared to live. He could read people: Carlos, the captain, our crew.

I was learning. I could feel these currents of faith, stay calmer, and even override some daily anxieties. It was hard to let go; completely let go. I still wanted some control, however

I did already realize this was the adventure of my life. We still had a long way to go; but I didn't worry about the captain or the crew. We would be just fine. I just enjoyed the images of the rays in my head while I slowly sipped on the last beer on our boat.

The captain, seemed eager to get home and punched the power. My body, exhausted from a day of fishing and snorkeling, started to recess into a fetal position. My eyes, tired and sore from being in water for over an hour, were heavy and ready to shut. Still, the mist of water from the front of the ship crashed into my face keeping me from falling asleep. I couldn't wait for my head to hit my pillow and my body to melt into my soft bed back at the hotel.

I gazed into the sky and noticed more clouds than blue sky overhead, but it really didn't concern me. It was still warm, however the weather seemed to be changing. If I wasn't so tired I might have cared more. The wind seemed to be picking up and making small waves that made our ride home a little bumpy.

I guess I was too tired to care. I enjoyed that last sip of my beer.

GROUNDED

We planned to fly out of La Paz tomorrow but those plans were in jeopardy. The second we returned to the Hotel Sol/Mar, Mike talked about the changing weather. The wind was picking up, blowing in dark clouds from the west. The local forecast, according to Mike, was ominous with three days of unsettled weather. Some rain, lots of wind and a sprinkle of sunshine mixed in. It would be hard to discern the exact time of a safe take-off.

Despite the troubling thoughts about the weather, once we reached our room, we crashed on our beds, dead from fatigue. Exhausted from our fishing and snorkeling excursion, we needed some time to recharge. My thoughts reflected on handing over my dorado to the hotel staff. They would clean, cut my fish, and put it on dry ice, securing its safe delivery home. I would enjoy it with my friends and family. That seemed so cool to me.

I questioned the fact that the fish would be good when got home. The staff assured me that it would survive the trip home. They warned me not to open the container until I was ready to cook the fish. It would be so fun to share the Dorado with my friends but we still had a long way to go. We were not going home anytime soon.

Late in my nap, over an hour old, I heard the first drops of rain. Lightly at the beginning, the rain gained in strength and intensity. I noticed Mike was already up and looking over the navigation map; reviewing our itinerary to Cabo. We needed only one more flight to reach our goal: Cabo San Lucas.

Mike said, "Nico, it's only fifty minutes, the shortest flight yet. Nice paved runway, no problem."

"Except the rain!" I exclaimed.

"Oh this will blow over. We just need a small fifty minute window of decent weather. I can get the plane up. We might not get into the air till the afternoon. We have to be ready when the opportunity presents itself." Mike lectured.

"Mike. I am not flying in the rain. I'm not flying in anything that looks risky. Do you catch my drift?" I calmly delivered.

"I catch your drift. I hear you. We'll ground the plane until we both feel comfortable with the conditions. Remember, you're my co-pilot." Mike reminded me.

"Now it's the weather! What's it gonna be next; locust, frogs, killer fog?" I bellowed.

"Hey, if God wants us grounded; we're grounded. He could be saving our lives, giving us sign not to fly. We have to discern when an opportunity will manifest itself and get out of here. Maybe God just wants us to spend a little more time in La Paz. I don't know; I just trust." Mike echoed his earlier faith responses.

"I wish I could feel your connection to God's wisdom and guidance. Sometimes, I think I'm in tune with God but it doesn't last long. Again, like in San Felipe; we don't take-off unless we both feel it's right. I don't mind waiting. Maybe God wants me to play my guitar again in the Harbor; I'm ready to ride this out." I responded.

My ears could hear the storm drains gurgling with new rain spilling down their spouts. The windows were wet and shrubs raked against the walls making a scraping sound. This storm came in quick. It caught us off guard. I was resolved; no flying in the wind and rain. We didn't need to take any chances; that's what God was relaying to my mind; no stupid decisions.

Mike brought up some facts. "We just need fifty minutes. A small window of time, really. However, the forecast didn't look favorable. We could be grounded for forty- eight hours.

Prophetically, two days later we were in the exact same position. The weather peppered the sky with black clouds, rain and strong winds. Nobody was flying except for the big jets. Twice, we had raced to the airport in the last two days, just to be disappointed when another squall forced us to retreat.

We were both getting frustrated and angry. We both started stretching the parameters, of our safety zones. Any fifty minute window that allowed us to get into the sky; light wind, light rain would be okay. I was softening my no- fly- in- rain stance. Drizzle would be fine now.

Finally, on the third day, a crack of blue sky pierced the gray sky. The winds were lighter and only a light drizzle dropped from the sky. The storm was breaking up; intermittent sun and light rain settled in around us.

Mike felt this was our chance. So, confident, we checked out of the Hotel Sol/Mar and bolted to the airport. It was nine in the morning and we could see more blue sky than clouds now. We powered up the plane, got clearance to take-off and rolled out onto the line-up. The runway was still damp from the morning rain but plenty dry for a safe take-off.

I watched other planes take-off with no trouble. I relaxed. We could do this. The airport was busy; in full swing as other planes wanted to get into the air as soon as possible. We were placed fourth in a line up; two jets, and two prop planes.

I had to ask the question, "Mike, will we face the same problems with jet-wash taking off behind a jet?"

"Not as bad." Mike stated, "The Jet is not reversing its engines to land, it's powering up to take off. Different set of physics. We should be okay."

"Should be okay?" What does that mean?" I shook my head.

"No worries Nico. It's almost our turn. Let's do this."

Mike focused on take off. A small prop took off in front of us easing my worries about taking off behind a jet. My calmness quickly turned to concern when the tower asked us to wait as a 737 landed. I pointed out our situation. "Mike, we are taking off behind a 737 that just landed. I can't believe this. We know what happened last time. What the hell is going on?"

"Nick, calm down. We'll wait long enough to let the jet wash dispense." Mike motioned to me that everything would be all right.

The tower gave us a verbal clearance to take off and Mike ignored it. We didn't move. Again, the tower asked us to depart. Again, the plane stayed still. Mike was sweating but stood firm. He grabbed the microphone and asked the tower for clearance; he was stalling. The air traffic controller's voice seeped of anger and he told Mike that he had already cleared Mike twice. He wanted to know if everything was all right. Mike smiled at me and whispered, "Do you think that's enough time?"

I smiled and gave him a big thumbs up sign; also shaking my head from head to toe. Mike told the terminal we were ready for take-off and launched the plane forward. The wheels spun up a trail of water and sped forward. The plane reacted beautifully; it was our sixth take off of the trip. We sailed into the air; Mike pointed the nose, south towards Cabo San Lucas. The adventure started anew. I was getting more relaxed in the air but I still felt anxiety creeping into my body.

However, how hard could fifty minutes be? I was used to the four hour variety. I reflected on what had transpired and realized we still had over half to go. Cabo San Lucas was supposed to be beautiful succulent, and intoxicating, one of the greatest vacation spots in the world. I couldn't wait to see all the wonders this place had to offer.

It was good to be flying again; in a strange way, I was beginning to like living on the edge. My body was relaxing earlier in the flight. I turned back to see La Paz, the largest city in Baja. La Paz, was the capital of Baja California Sur. Baja held five municipalities that comprise the 32 Federal entities or states, of Mexico. Cabo San Lucas, one of the most famous vacation spots in the world, not to mention the fishing, was located at its southern tip.

The weather was semi-dry, almost Mediterranean. Out of nowhere I asked Mike if Father Junipero Serra did missionary work in Baja. I knew Serra blanketed the west coast with missions.

"Yes, Nick. I believe around 1768 or so. In fact all three major missionary groups have been in Baja. The Jesuits were first, then Franciscans, that was Junipero Serra's group, and finally Dominicans. During their colonial period, everyone was trying to evangelize the people. It's still very Catholic."

"Wow, someone has done his homework." I was impressed.

"Yeah, I studied a lot before we came. Like to know as much as possible about the place I'm flying into. Makes for more of an adventure; don't you think?"

I just shook my head. "Thanks for the history lesson. I guess Junipero Serra got around. We have a mission in Santa Cruz, a mission in Carmel."

Mike jumped in, "The missions are all over our diocese.

Heck, all over the state. Anyhow, Cabo is supposed to be incredible. We will be there in no time. Shortest flight yet!"

I could not wait to see the beauty of this place. Our final destination, our goal, was within reach. It wouldn't take long now. A sense of accomplishment caressed our bodies as we crept toward Cabo. We had made it. Or so we thought.

HURRICANE

Mike dodged the clouds like he was avoiding poison oak, and for good reason. Every time we flew through the billowy mass of charged particles the turbulence was extreme. The plane would drop suddenly, be pushed sideways or shake as though experiencing a mild earthquake.

I helped Mike find blue cracks in the sky and asked him to drop some altitude. I always felt more relaxed at 7,500 feet but that's exactly where some clouds have their greatest effect. We dropped to 2,500, with very few low clouds, however, we were met by a strong headwind. It was anything but smooth but at least the plane wasn't shaking so bad.

"These headwinds will push the trip to over an hour." Mike stated.

"No problem. Just don't go through any big clouds. It feels like we're fighting the air." I exclaimed.

"I think we can make it without any more problems. It's pretty broken up. It's just a straight line to Cabo now." Mike was always so positive.

"Cabo Wabo", I echoed.

The rest of the ride was uneventful and we spotted the airport easily. Before Mike headed for final approach he decided to fly over our hotel and the beautiful bay surrounding it. The color of the water; turquoise that seemed to radiate a fiery blue glow. This efflorescent glow stretched into the deeper blue water and gave the bay a two tone splash of color. Beautiful boats lined the Harbor; four-star hotels littered the beaches. It was spectacular.

However, another view caught our eyes. Just across the street from the Harbor was a row of slums. Cardboard houses. No paved streets; linen blowing in the wind providing shelter from the weather. Poverty; pushed against luxury. A depressing sight. Only the paved road divided these two different worlds.

I felt remorse, almost shame that I was going to the money side. We were staying at a four star hotel on the beach. Yet, directly across the street people struggled to survive. A strange twist of fate separated us. The tent city stretched on for miles.

"Mike look, only a road separates prestige and power from poverty. You think with all the tourist money they could help their own people. The poor peasants. All they have to do is look across the street; huge hotels, fancy cars, giant fishing boats, swimming pools." I could feel their pain.

"We have to keep them in our prayers." Mike said as he shook his head. "Now let's go land this bird."

We made contact with the terminal and Mike preceded to land on a nice paved runway. The airport housed over fifty planes; mostly private jets and props. Mike greased his second landing in a row and reached out to give me a high five. "We made it! Cabo San Lucas. I knew we could do this. The odds were with us you know.

"Cabo Wabo." I belted out. "What do you mean the odds were with us?"

Silence. We were slowly taxing from the runway to the tarmac when both of us had the same discovery! Every plane we passed was tied down. Ropes were wrapped around all parked planes anchoring them tightly to the ground. It was eerie. Mike spoke first. "These people are expecting some rough weather."

"Maybe this is a response to the last storm?" I brought up.

"I don't think so." Mike observed. "They would be untying them if that was true. This looks serious. We better find out what's going on."

We found a spot to park the plane and immediately went searching for some answers. Three planes down from us a man was tying his plane down. I ran in front of Mike and asked him, "What's going on?"

"Hurricane." That's all he said.

Hurricane?" Mike joined in almost out of breath.

"Sixty miles southwest. It could slam into us any time after midnight. It could also miss us altogether. Can't take any chances. No one knows. You should tie your plane down. We'll get 50-70 mile per hour winds; maybe stronger. Personally, I think it will miss us but it's going to be one hell of night!"

ONE HELL OF A NIGHT

We tied the plane down with help from Aaron, a pilot we just met. We didn't have any rope but Aaron offered his extra and helped us anchor the plane to the ground. He told us that hurricanes didn't generally hit Cabo San Lucas. Most, fizzled out and ran up the west coast of Baja. He could sense the worry in our faces, "Don't stress too much about this. Tonight will be rough, but we'll still be here in the morning."

Mike jumped in, "I should have been more on top of this weather. It kinda sneaked up on us. A hurricane is a serious event."

"Let's get to the hotel" I joined in.

It started to rain; the wind was picking up too. The hotel was a short distance from the airport. We checked in and all the staff had down-played the hurricane.

"We have generators. No problems." said the manager who was assuring all the new guests that the hotel was ready for anything.

Our room, nestled right against the sand, had a small kitchen and bath with a shower overlooking the beach. Only a seawall was between the Cabo sand and our room. It was a beach bungalow. The waves were already crashing onto the shore and the wind was picking up. Something ominous was coating the air; I could feel its intensity. We had to prepare for a long night and I didn't feel too comfortable having nothing but a seawall between me and the ocean. How far would the water come in?

Our vacation evolved back into an adventure. My fight or flight response to stress was back and I cautioned Mike against what we needed to prepare for, "Mike. Are we safe here? Ocean surges are unpredictable and happen during Hurricanes. What do you think?"

Mike, as positive as ever, said, "Nico, this thing isn't coming onshore. I talked to the bartender when we walked through the lobby."

"Not the bartender again." I rolled my eyes.

"Yep! The bartender said we'll be okay. Winds over 50 but the hurricane is spinning itself out. It will be downgraded to a tropical storm before it hits land. Plus, it's heading up the west coast; away from us." Mike reported.

"That's nice." I smiled.

Mike finished, "The bartender says that after tomorrow the weather will be fabulous!"

The lights started to flicker on and off before nine. The force of the wind caused the plants outside to scratch the sides of the bungalow. The sound was disturbing but the howling noise of the wind was even more uncomfortable. The gust of wind surely reached over 50mph. The sound from the waves breaking against the rocks shook the room. A giant storm; centered directly above us, showed off its power sounding goaded by anger.

"How long do you think before the lights go off?" I offered.

"No problem. I got these candles from the manager." Mike proudly exclaimed.

We lit the candles and tried to read our books and stay calm. The lights flickered steadily and I was surprised they lasted till midnight. Rain and wind pelted our room and didn't let up until three in the morning. I couldn't sleep; it was pitch black, and all I could hear were the waves crashing upon our seawall. I was worried the water would find a way into our room. However, it did seem like the storm was losing some intensity. It was quieter and I could hear less scratching on the siding of our bungalow. I finally feel asleep around three. Mike seemed unfazed by the storm, snoring loudly for the last few hours. Nothing seemed to rattle Mike, he just rolled with the punches of life.

Even during my dream state, I worried about a giant rogue wave, crashing down on our room. I could hear the waves pounding the shore and racing towards the seawall that protected the front of our room. Another thunderous splashing sound was heard when the water crashed into the rocks just left of our room.

The wind seemed to be getting stronger again, blowing the rain sideways against our windows. I felt the ground shake, it seemed the whole building was being pulled into the ocean. We were caught in a giant rip tide.

Mike shook my shoulder and shouted, "Wake up Nick. Wake up. You're dreaming. Hey get this. The beach in front of our room is gone!"

"What time is it? What's gone?" I groggily spit out

"It's seven. And the beach is gone. Come check it out!" Mike bellowed.

I could not believe it was seven. My whole body felt disoriented, but I remembered the dream. We were being pulled out. I thought about the dream as I dressed. Mike nearly pulled me out the door.

The sea wall had sunk sideways about six feet; it slid down to the level of the beach. The strangest sight was looking out at the beach. It was gone. The waves pulled all the sand out to sea. A giant crater fifty yards wide remained, filled with nothing but wet sand. It was a ten foot drop straight down from the crumbling seawall, with no way to get back up. The enormous hole replaced the beautiful beach. It would take months to recover.

The second strange thing was the calmness of the weather. Blue sky filled the air, only a soft wind blew and it was starting to get hot. All the guests at the hotel drank their morning coffee looking out at the once prestigious land. All conversations revolved around the storm and what could have been. The big stuff missed us, I could only imagine what damage it could have caused. The power was still out. I could hear the generators powering up.

We had a chance to enjoy a hot breakfast. Mike brought up something I totally forgot about, "We have to get to the plane. If this storm could bring down a seawall, it could tip over a plane."

"I forgot about the plane. I don't know how but I forgot about the plane." I said forgetting our most important asset; transportation.

"I didn't forget about my plane, Nico. Let's get something to eat and make our way to the plane. Hey, did I snore last night?"

Mike always asked me if he snored last night. I answered, "You snore every night Mike."

Mike reflected, "I always sleep better when it's raining."

"It was a freaking hurricane Mike. A hurricane!" I said.

"I slept like a baby." Mike laughed.

How could he sleep? I certainly couldn't. In fact, I didn't sleep till well into the morning. My mind, currently foggy, retained the sounds of the hurricane. They were ominous, and had kept me frightened for most of the night. Mike, on the other hand, had total confidence in the storm heading North and away from us.

I wasn't so sure. Was this a lack of faith or my Virgo worry-wort syndrome kicking into overdrive? I mean, you have to be practical. I had every right to be on high alert, concerned! We all did.

At present, the sun was met by nothing but blue sky. The clouds had scattered elsewhere and a beautiful day was being born. The drastic change in weather was perplexing. So dangerous one second; so docile the next. This part of the world was interesting. I had never seen such a sudden change. However, I liked the new change.

My thoughts raced to the Archer II. If it was damaged we would be stranded here for some time. I didn't like those images; I had things to do at home. I was running a couple of basketball camps that needed me there. I also imagined seeing the plane broken in two. The tail bent sideways and dislodged from the fuselage. The wings snapped off and cracked. The front window with a tree through the glass.

Suddenly, what really worried me! My prized guitar was on board. It better not be cracked.

DID IT FLIP OVER?

The ride to the airport turned quiet and somber. Our eyes surveyed the aftermath of the storm with concern and uncertainty. Trees had fallen, limbs and leaves littered across the road and a long line of traffic greeted us as we merged onto the only road headed for the airport. A short 20 minute trip turned into a forty minute creep; too many cars. Traffic signals were out and out taxi driver kept cussing and shaking his fist at the traffic he encountered.

Mike was worried about the plane. He said, "I hope it didn't flip over. I bet most of this traffic holds pilots anxious to get to their planes."

"That would be us. I have my fingers crossed." I showed Mike my hands.

"Nick if the plane is damaged and repairs are needed we might be here longer than we anticipated." Mike pointed out.

"I know you have prayers for planes?" I smiled. "Especially, yours!"

"We can't just pray for our plane," Mike stated and blessed himself and continued, "God please, no damage to anyone's plane. Especially ours. You know which one it is."

"Wow, that was deep. Amen." I tried to down play the intensity of the moment. We both blessed ourselves and hoped for the best.

I could finally see the turn off to the airport. Traffic had nearly come to a stand-still. Mike was right; the pilots were all checking their planes. It took another twenty minutes to get to the access road that would take us to our plane. However, we could already see some damage. Mike pointed and said, "Look at that."

A plane had tipped over and was flat on its back. In fact, I could see four other planes either flipped over or on their sides. The tarmac was full of pilots assessing the damage. I strained to look forward to see our plane. My eyes glazed over when I saw our plane perfectly upright and looking amazingly solid. Our ropes held. We were lucky. "Unbelievable" Mike shook his head and rubbed his hand across the side of the plane. "Not a scratch. I love this plane." Mike finished.

We carefully inspected the plane and couldn't find any damage. Ten other planes flipped; we didn't. Why? Was God watching over us? Protecting us? Other pilots prayed for their planes, I'm sure. However, many of them were disappointed. Did God answer our prayer but not theirs?

I asked Mike, "Why did our plane survive? Did God bless us?"

"No." Mike jumped straight in, "Nick check it out. All the planes that flipped over were high wing planes. All the low wings survived. I think it was basic physics. It was easier for the wind to pick up the high wing planes and move them around. The design of our plane saved it. Oh yeah, God helps everyone in one way or another. He has truly blessed us on this trip. This adventure will have lasting memories forever!" Mike smiled.

We spent most of the afternoon trying to help other pilots. Only four of the ten planes seemed heavily damaged. It seemed but a few minutes when planes started taking off with regularity.

We didn't notice the power was back on until we got back from the airport.

I headed straight for a hot shower and met Mike for dinner in the hotel's restaurant. Everything seemed to return to normal but I was quickly reminded of the turmoil we encountered with last night's storm when I glanced out to the beach. I saw a sunken seawall; a ten foot drop, and no beach. Beauty, shockingly destroyed. I remembered how pretty it was just a few hours earlier. We were blessed again. We were alive, unhurt, and in good health. Our plane was standing solid.

I glanced at the damage to other parts of the hotel. The entire staff seemed to be working overtime. Every corner of the property needed cleaning. Small limbs, and thousands of leaves littered the walkways. Both Mike and I needed some time to relax. Cabo San Lucas was our goal. We were 1,480 miles from home and filled when a sense of accomplishment.

It was time for the adventure to turn into the vacation: Swimming pools, hot sun, snorkeling, fishing, and falling asleep in the shade by our room. Still, it was odd we no longer had a beach. It looked great in the brochure; too bad it was gone. We had three days of great weather in front of us. Cabo was going to be nice; we just had to give it some time.

CRUISE SHIP

The night was quiet and cool. Fresh air permeated our rooms and made sleeping easy. I was so tired my body felt petrified when my head hit the pillow; a wonderful feeling. Last night, I didn't sleep at all so I was looking forward to a long restful sleep. Mike's snoring didn't even bother me; my hearing receptors were too tired to listen. My thoughts replayed last night's storm and all the sounds it created.

Tonight, quiet and peaceful, I enjoyed the silence. Tomorrow we would journey to Cabo Bay Harbor. With a little luck we could see a giant cruise ship and search out a couple of good snorkeling spots. We only had two days left and I wanted to make the most of our time here. We already lost three days because of the weather

Our morning was postponed until after nine; we both slept in. Strange for Mike, normal for me. After breakfast, we headed into town and eventually to the Harbor. It was horseshoe shaped, cut perfectly out of the rock that rimmed the Harbor. Beautiful. The size and dimensions brought almost artistic grace to the landscape. The water, a combination of various shades of blue, seemed luminescent. My eyes scanned the entrance to the Harbor and saw what I wanted to see, "Mike look! A cruise ship."

"Yea, Royal Caribbean," Mike pointed out. "It's fifteen

stories high; has an 800 seat theater, and one whole deck is just a shopping mall."

"Unreal!" I admired the ship.

The ship as anchored 100 yards from the entrance to the harbor. Any boat leaving would have to venture very close to the titanic ship. I wanted to be on one of those boats.

"Mike, let's get on a fishing boat so we can get close to that cruise ship."

"I guess you really like that ship. All right, let's make it happen." Mike walked briskly toward the boats.

The only boat we could get on was a snorkeling boat that took half a day. I had no problem with that; I loved to snorkel, but better yet, we would have to travel right by the cruise ship. I was amazed at Mike's ability to adjust to life's little curve balls and roll with the flow. I think he wanted to fish but never hesitated to get on the snorkeling boat.

We boarded and headed out slowly with about eight other tourists. Mike and I would have to share this boat. My eyes were fixated on the cruise ship right in front of us. We ran almost parallel to the giant ship for a good 5 minutes. What a treat. The scope of the ship seemed to defy physics. To me, this was the 747 of the ocean. How could something that big be built? How did it float? I guess Noah's Ark had some incredible size, but not like this. I fantasized about getting on a ship of that size and cruising the world.

"Nico, it's incredible." Mike gazed at the ship. "A giant toast to human engineering. I bet it holds three thousand; ten heated swimming pools and enough food for months. Nico, someday! However, I think I would prefer to fly!" Mike winked.

"Nothing personal. I love flying," I sarcastically stated, "But my next trip is going to be on a giant cruise ship."

"You'll have to fly to catch one of these in LA or Alaska." Mike pointed out.

"I was thinking the Mediterranean." I schooled Mike.

"That's a long flight. 10 hours. My Piper can't make it across the Atlantic."

"Mike I'll be on a giant plane. A 747." I said.

The snorkeling trip was great but also a disappointment compared to La Paz. No ray or turtles. Lots of fish, small, yet colorful. The best part were the reefs. The coral was on fire with color. Yellow, red, green and blue flashed upward from the bottom. The biggest disappointment was not seeing the giant cruise ship when we returned.

It must have left just hours before. I felt a bit stung by the empty spot where the ship anchored. I really wanted to see it again. The drive home was unusually quiet. Mike had been hinting to me to get ready for some change of plans. I could see he was calculating something in his head. His lips were moving but no sound was made. What new surprise was he conjuring up? I would find out soon.

SURPRISE!

"Nico, I think we should go further south." Mike brought up, "Do you think you could handle a couple of extra days? In fact, three extra days added to our trip?"

He was hiding information. I challenged him, "All right. The only thing south of us is water. What are you thinking?"

Mike calmly stated, "I booked us on a ferry to Mazatlan. It will add three extra days to our trip. Is that okay?"

Truthfully, I want to get back home. I was starting to get homesick. The crazy flights, out of control planes, dirt landings, Montezuma's revenge had left me drained. However, a voice deep in my consciousness told me it would be all right. Mike was excited, he was my friend and I had to support his vacation. Plus, a trip to Mazatlan. Mike was generous, I answered, "I've never been to Mazatlan. I'm in. Sounds great. When do we leave?"

"Hold on. I will confirm our reservations tonight. It's not a cruise ship; I wish it was. We do have inside cabins on the ferry." Mike stated.

"Sounds great!" I interrupted.

Mike jumped back in, "Okay, the peasants ride back and forth on this ship. We were lucky to get inside cabins. We can only buy one way tickets so as soon as we reach Mazatlan we have to buy return tickets. Shouldn't be a problem."

"How long does it take?" I questioned

"One whole night. But less than 24hrs." Mike pretended to add the hours as he talked.

Once again I said, "That sounds doable. I'm in."

Mike raised his hand and finally got to the problem. "We have to leave the plane here, drive back to La Paz and catch the ferry."

"In La Paz?" I mentioned.

"In La Paz." Mike returned.

"But we're in Cabo San Lucas." I lectured.

"Yea, It's an hour and a half drive. If we leave early we have plenty of time to catch the ferry by eleven. Are you still in? I got a hotel in Mazatlan reserved; right on the water." Mike grinned.

"I'm in," I said with some force, "Hey, why can't we just fly?" I was searching for an easier option.

"Can't fly. This is one time it's easier and faster to drive. We can drive straight to the dock; get out, and board the ferry, just before it leaves. If we fly, it's still a long drive to the dock from the La Paz airport. We have to drive to make this work. I've flown us all the way down here, you can drive back to La Paz." Mike winked.

It all made sense but seemed silly. No matter, Mazatlan was our new goal. I would call home and alert my girlfriend and my mother.

My girlfriend was happy for me; my mother was going to be the tough one. Once I said hi to my mother she took off. "Hi Son, how are you doing? I haven't got a card yet from you; you've been sending them, haven't you?"

"Off course mom; I can't believe you haven't got one yet." I was lying but I was trapped in a corner. I continued, "Anyway mom, we're going to Mazatlan! It's a south of where we are so I'm going to be three days late getting back."

My mother said, "Who's paying for that? Are you flying?"

Before I could answer one question she started again, "Nick I have been praying to the Sacred Heart of Jesus. I have lit candles. Now, I'm saying the Rosary. I am guessing you've had a pretty good trip so far, huh?

I was too tired to go into what had transpired in the last few days. I knew an easy way out of the conversation and I took it, "Mom, thanks for your thoughts and prayers. I'm sure they are helping us. The trip has gone so smoothly you can't believe it. The plane is running great and Father Cross is a great pilot. Please, don't worry about us, I'll see you soon. I'll try to find out what happened to those post cards. I'm sure you'll get yours any day now."

My mom had the last word. "Oh, that's great news. Tell Father Cross everything in the parish is going great too. Can't wait to see you. Love you, thanks for calling." As I hung up the phone I realized that maybe my Mom was helping us.

Prayers are powerful. Were my mom's prayers keeping us safe? The luck that we had so far seemed more like fate. A path of adventure that was unfolding in front of us. If I told her the truth she would have stressed even more.

I walked directly over to Mike and asked, "Do you have people praying for us; I mean for this trip?"

"Off course. Prayers probably have kept us alive; and a good pilot. Anyhow, why?"

"My mom is praying too! I think those prayers have helped."

Mike smiled and spoke firmly, "Those prayers will get us all the way home. However, we have a little trek further south. What's the farthest south you ever made?"

"Mazatlan. This is it Mike. How cool is that?"

"Oh, it's hot in Mazatlan, Nick."

We were both venturing further South than we ever had

in our lives. My mind shot back to the image of lot's of people praying for Mike and me. Somehow, we were all connected; all sending out energy to each other. I said a silent prayer of thanks for them; and worked with Mike on the logistics of getting to the ferry.

Mike needed to make preparations with both the ferry and a Mazatlan Hotel. He would be on the phone for some time. I sneaked in a quick shower and grabbed my guitar. The patio would be a perfect place to play.

Still, my mind couldn't let go of the images of all the people praying for us; supporting us. My mom, maybe my girlfriend, all of St. Joseph's staff and maybe half the parishioners. I tried to add up people and stopped when I realized it could be over 200 people. I thought we were alone here but you could feel the prayers, the spirituality of people that prayed, some that didn't even know us.

I was cared for. So many prayers, so much good fortune. Everything that happened to us so far wasn't a coincidence.

Mike kept saying, "If God wanted us dead, we would be dead."

That made sense to me. After all, every breath I take is dependent on God. I can't even hold my breath till I die; God won't let that happen. I have to make a conscious effort, from my own free will, to hurt myself. I am at the mercy of the Natural Laws set upon planet Earth by God.

This trip was opening up concepts and ideas that had eluded me. Spiritual thoughts were challenging me. I was changing.

I looked at Mike and from nowhere asked him about his vocation. When he heard God's call. I don't know why I asked him but Mike didn't hesitate.

"I wanted to become a priest so I wouldn't have to work!" Mike, always the humorist.

"Okay, very funny. I know that priests work very hard. I mean, when did you decide to become a priest so you didn't have to work?" I questioned with my own humor.

Mike's eyes blinked and he turned to the side away from me. He looked out past the patio; almost out to sea. He smiled and turned back to me and said, "You sure you want to hear it? It's simple to me yet very complicated."

I came right back, "Of course, I want to hear it!"

Mike gulped down some air and came right back, "I went to high school in Bakersfield. It was a Catholic High school run by the Christian Brothers; Garces High School. I was a junior when it happened!"

"What happened?" I interrupted.

Mike continued, "Like I said I was a junior; maybe 15 or 16. I wasn't that great a student though I was making the grade. One day I was sitting in class, I believe it was a history class, when a 'call slip' came for me. I had never got a 'call slip' before so I thought that maybe I was in trouble. I was asked to meet a priest who wanted to see me in the main office. Very odd, but heck it got me out of the class. I jumped up and headed off straight away.

I entered the office and was led to a room with a priest waiting for me that I did not recognize. I pretty much knew all the priests so this was disconcerting but I walked up to him and told him my name. The priest immediately asked if I would be interested in going to Seminary Days. It was like a retreat for those interested in joining the priesthood.

He said I would be a good candidate and seemed very excited for me. He explained I could join what was called a minor seminary for my senior year. It was for candidates who had not graduated from high school yet. If I liked the school I could move on to a major Seminary and then on to Ryan Prep

College and eventually to St. John's seminary. After that it could be four years of theology but it all ended with me joining the priesthood. It sound great to me but at the time I wasn't sure where my life might go. I thanked him and headed back to class. I was certainly excited by the possibilities."

"Do you remember the priests name?" I blurted out.

"Well, that's where it gets a little strange." Mike's eyebrows raised. "After some thought I went back to the office to find out the priest's name. He never mentioned his name. No one in the office knew who he was. It was a mystery."

I started rambling, "Wait a minute. How did he get into the office? You have to check in. You just can't summon a student out of class without credentials!"

"I know." Mike agreed. "But to this day, he is a mystery in my life. I immediately contacted everyone in the office; including the principal. No one could identify him. In fact, no one even remembered him being in the building!"

"Incredible!" I shouted. "Maybe a guardian angel" I surmised.

"Yes, and No." Mike spoke, "Perhaps a messenger; that's what I have come to realize.

Certainly an Angel. Perhaps my guardian angel. It all happened so fast."

"That's incredible." I couldn't stop saying that.

Yeah, but later, a second angel entered my life and made sure I finished my schooling.", Mike said.

"A second angel? I questioned.

"Yes, and his name was 'Big Jim'" Mike lit up as he spoke.

"Angels have names like 'Big Jim'" I only knew of Gabriel and Michael.

"Yeah, 'Big Jim'" Mike said confidently. "You see, I could have never afforded the tuition. The cost of the seminary, plus four years of theology at Cammillo is not cheap. We were poor. My sister went into the convent. My brother went oversea. It was just my mom and me. We were struggling to survive; we had no money.

My father died at 52; my mom could never afford the cost of sending me to the seminary. 'Big Jim' took us both under his wing; helped mom with bills and helped pay for my schooling. Truly, I might not have gone down that path without his help. He was like a father to me. He filled a huge hole in my life. I owe him so much!"

"A second guardian angel; you were blessed. You should write a book about this. Amazing!" I was dumbfounded. "So is 'Big Jim' an old family friend?"

"I guess you could say that but he was so much more. My first contact was on a paper route when I was a kid. He also knew my Dad. Long story short, yes, a person I will never forget." Mike's eyes could hardly hold the tears that were generated by a very powerful relationship.

"Yeah, someday, a book. I've always thought about it." Mike turned serious.

"That is a great story Mike. Surely you were meant to be a priest" I shook my head.

The rest of the afternoon we talked about how God sometimes really uses angels to influence our decisions. Mike pointed out that after that experience he always had a place in his heart for guardian angels. He felt everyone had an angel that looked after them and tried to guide them to make good decisions. He would point out that they influence our life and we should pray to them.

Apparently they do have quite an effect on our lives. At least, it seemed they double teamed Father Cross.

WHERE'S THE CHURCH?

Mike was frustrated when he found out the ferry didn't leave on Sundays until 2pm. On the other hand, I was relieved. We didn't have to rush off, we could sleep in.

Tomorrow was Sunday. My Catholic programing, so perfectly practiced, figured we would be going to church tomorrow. It was right on the way to the harbor, I saw it; Madonna del Sasso Catholic Church. We could go to the 8 am mass and easily make it to La Paz, long before departure.

I was excited to experience the local spirituality. I figured I would see a traditional mass; probably in spanish. Mike never talked about going to mass and it was getting late in the evening so I brought it up, "Hey Mike. We hitting the church in the morning?"

"Oh, yeah, church." Mike smirked. "We are on vacation. I almost forgot about mass. You know Nick, I was so totally caught up in this adventure I forgot about going to church. I certainly want to thank God for this adventure. Boy has he looked out for us. Besides, every church community is different. It could be fun!"

"I've never thought the Mass was fun." I stared at Mike.

Certainly, few Catholics find the Mass fun. In fact, many would call it boring, repetitive, and cold. However, I have seen communities that have the Holy Spirit. It is alive and thriving.

Relationships branch out and many are touched. The Mass is a holy celebration of life. The whole assembly of gathered people, radiating love and being uplifted. I looked forward to Mass tomorrow; I couldn't wait to experience what I would feel and see.

When we woke up it was dark and overcast. The wind was freshening and a chill sat in the air. We packed and threw everything inside the rental car and headed for the church; just a short drive from our hotel. It was modest in size with four stained glass windows.

The church built in the shape of a cross. The outside design was nothing special but fabulous on the inside. When you crossed the entrance you ran right into the most beautiful fountain, a baptismal font. The water poured out of what seemed like solid rock. Spectacular! When the local people passed by, they would dip their fingers in the water and bless themselves. We could hear them say three different prayers, "In the name of the Father, and of the Son, and of the Holy Spirit. Forgive me father! Cleanse me from my Sin. Renew my Baptism"

I kept listening; so did Mike. My God, they said all their prayers out loud! Everyone could hear. I just watched in amazement. They would throw water onto their foreheads as if John the Baptist himself was gently pouring water out of the Jordan. I liked that image. They were renewing their baptism in a way that the early converts did when they approach John for baptism. Mixing history and tradition always entices and affects me.

I finally walked up and put my fingers over the water and caught a nice amount on my fingertips. I wiped my forehead and felt John the Baptist's spirit touch me. The water splashed on my forehead and I started the sign of the cross. I glanced down at my shirt and noticed it was wet from my fingers. I must have really got more water than I thought.

Mike simply blessed himself with the sign of the cross. He loved this; I could tell. This church was alive. You could feel it. We rushed to find some seats, the church was filling up. I grabbed Mike and pulled him to two seats I saw in the front row. Perfect. Old wooden pews with soft pads for kneeling. Four sets of pews, ten rows deep, faced each other around an altar in the middle. The people surrounded the Tabernacle.

The altar was surrounded equally on four sides. Nice design. It looked like local musicians made up a band of ten. Drums, guitars, keyboards and percussive instruments were warmed up and ready to go. They hit the entrance song and the whole congregation rose into song. Everyone sang. Everyone clapped their hands and raised their hands to the Lord. The Spirit was alive in this community.

Mike and I looked at each other and got involved. We sang and clapped until our hands got sore. Good Lord! I was having fun. Miracle. I always think miracle when God communicates with me. I said you can't have fun at Church. God said, "Yes you can."

The priest said the opening prayers in both Spanish and English. His sermon was about letting God lead; connect to his power. I was learning on this trip that God has a connection with each of us and let's us decide how much we want to engage. It seemed the greater commitment is to start that relationship with God. That connection has incredible power to change people's lives and do mighty things. I wanted to stay connected to God's spirit. I could feel the strength of the Spirit in this church.

Communion was quiet, holy and respectful. Each person I saw made the sign of the cross after communion. I liked that.

I was getting some new ideas. I liked these new movements. I would take them home with me and share their influence on me. Maybe others would start these traditions in our church back home.

After mass, we talked to the priest about our journey. He grabbed and pulled us aside. He presided to give us a special blessing. He invited others to put their hands on us while he prayed. I could feel the warmth of the people around us. Was this the holy spirit? The blessing took a couple of minutes to finish. Mike thanked him and the last thing I heard him say was "Father Mike, safe and happy landings. God bless both of you."

We made the sign of the cross and thanked Father Henry. "Wow that was intense!" Mike said walking to the car.

"Wow! I was feeling the Spirit. Big Time!" I excitedly proclaimed.

"Me too!" Mike blew air out of his mouth. "We almost missed it. Thanks for reminding me about mass."

"I wasn't sure if you folks take Sundays off on vacation." I stated.

"Yes Nick, sometimes we do. But I'm so glad we had that mass experience. I want to take that energy back to our parish. I wish our community could celebrate like that!" Mike said in deep thought.

"It will Mike. It will." I said with confidence.

From my past church experience, it didn't take me long to figure out that a church community took on the personality of its pastor. Whatever spirituality the pastor brought into church; the parish evoked the same trait. As long as you could preach, the church was in your hands. However, if you couldn't preach, you could lose most of the congregation. I learned, some Catholic's would stay no matter what; others would move to other local churches. If the priest lacked relational skills, and appeared lacking in spirituality, he could be run out of town. Of course, if you could raise money, the Bishop would always have a job for you.

Father Cross had been given perhaps the flag ship of the Monterey diocese: St. Joseph's. I had been a member since I was five. I had seen three priests come and go. I witnessed the destruction of the original property; an old and falling apart building to its new pristine property.

Back at the old church, I was Father John Kennedy's alter server. He was the first priest I heard swear, on a golf course. He let me see him as a human being. It was refreshing. He was also responsible for the new St. Joseph's. Father Kennedy started a fund raising drive that lasted for years. Finally, we had enough to hold the loan on a new church; the property less than half a mile from our present building.

Father Kennedy gave his parishioners, who were donating so much money, a chance to design the new church. One person wanted a long tunnel; others wanted huge stained glass windows. Another wanted the entire building to be built in the shape of a cross.

The architect, with father Kennedy infused many of these ideas. I am proud to say I was a part of that History. Though I had no major impact on the building; my ideas were heard; along with everyone else. Father Kennedy realized the importance of being connected.

The people of St. Joseph's have always poured their hearts out to welcome its priest. Father Mike worked hard to make St. Joseph's special. He worked with the parish council and ran the church well. The people generally embraced him and welcomed him. Father Mike wanted to be relational; more approachable.

I think this is what Mike saw in this church 1,480 miles

away. Everyone seemed connected. The spirituality of each person shined forth. No one wants to be in a spirituality dead church. It must be a nightmare for a parish priest. I figured that job number one of a new priest was to create a spirit of joy, peace and safety. Hopefully God gave Mike the skills to do it. At least, he wanted it. I wanted to believe in him. It was great having him as a friend.

Mike let me drive all the way to La Paz. Very bumpy, but we made it on time. I could see the ferry off in the distance. It was actually fairly big. This was going to be fun.

THE FERRY

"Holy Cow!", Mike projected as he gazed out to the giant Ferry.

"What?", I was clueless as I reached for our luggage.

"It's an automobile ferry. No wonder it's so cheap." Mike scratched his head. "Look at all the cars lined up to board!"

Mike pointed to perhaps 50 cars anxiously waiting to proceed on the ship. In fact, a line of over 100 people circled the dock. This ship appeared to have multiple jobs. A car ferry, and a people ferry.

Mike and I waited in line for over an hour before actually getting to our cabin. The room was small but my bed was comfortable. We unpacked and quickly headed to the top deck to watch the ferry disembark. The outside decks and walk ways were almost full of people just sitting and waiting. They looked tired and stiff from standing in line for many hours. It almost seemed that they were getting ready to camp.

"Mike, what are they doing? Did they overbook?", I questioned.

Mike thought for a second and then explained, "No, Nick. The Sunday ferry is a gateway for the locals to move back and forth. Cheap transportation to Mazatlan. The ferry lets these people sit out here, sleep out here, hell, live out here for almost 18 hours. They give these people a great conduit to Mazatlan at a great price. The grateful passengers are happy for the ride.

They don't care about the conditions. The warm salt air moistens their senses. Look, they brought sandwiches and water."

I surveyed the mass of people and spoke, "Isn't some safety rule being broken?"

"No rules here Nico. Just a ferry company making all the money it can. Economics! Mere Economics my friend." Mike bellowed.

"You mean Mere Christianity; C.S. Lewis." I proudly pointed out. I had just read Lewis's book before the trip.

"Pure Economics. You got it." Mike finished.

We soon learned the ferry had few inside rooms. In fact, very few cabins even existed. I almost felt embarrassed we had such a nice room. We later found out most of the people who boarded in cars just stayed in them. Instant hotel. From my point of view, the ferry was a commuter bus packed to the gills with locals making a daily or weekly trek. I saw very few tourists perhaps only a handful. We stuck out; the locals were checking us out as much as we watched them. Mike was smart to pick up sandwiches before we boarded. The ferry provided only water and bathrooms. This was a bare bones ship. No amenities. Just transportation.

We sailed out of La Paz about 20 minutes late. The ship listed rhythmically, back and forth. This deviation from the vertical would rock me to sleep tonight. However, just before getting ready for bed I crept out to the outside decks and sidewalks to see how the people were doing. Curiosity had got hold of me and I wanted to see how comfortable the decks really were.

To my surprise; no complaining. Almost silence. Living on hard decks outside didn't seem to bother anyone. This could never happen in America. Some ordinance would be broken. They would force the people into another area. However, here, just outside La Paz, in the Sea of Cortez, these people could sit wherever they wanted.

I glanced up to the sky to check the weather. A sudden storm could manifest a dreadful night for these people. My eyes only saw stars. It was clear and warm. The moon light shined on the water guiding our path. It almost seemed romantic; except for the situation. I felt many of them had done this many times before; they just seemed so calm and comfortable, so quiet. They smiled at me and curled up in blankets. I still thought it was an amazing sight.

Once convinced that they were going to be fine, I headed back to our cabin. I was feeling a little seasick as I winded down some stairs and down a corridor. The nausea had sneaked up on me. Mike was already asleep and snoring like a rocket. I jumped on my bed and stretched out. I was tired. It didn't take long for the sickness to subside and the relaxation of sleep to begin.

We would be in Mazatlan in the morning; practically when we woke up. The only thing I knew about Mazatlan was the United States invaded it in 1948-49 during the Mexican/American War. I also read the American western hero, actor, movie star, John Wayne would vacation in Mazatlan on fishing expeditions with his pals. It must be nice.

MAZATLAN

We were approaching the Mazatlan Harbor. Mike shook my shoulder back and forth and almost shouted, "Wake up. We are close enough to see land. Get up! We want to be topside as we get closer!"

I was being awakened from a deep sleep; only one of my eyes popped open. I could hear Mike but could not respond. My head whipped back and forth and I shouted, "I'm up! I'm up." I now realized where I was and continued, "I'm right behind you. What time is it?"

"It's seven-thirty. I've been up for an hour. Come on let's go. Mazatlan awaits!" Mike spoke with nervous energy.

I jumped up, dressed faster than a fireman and sprinted out of the room just two steps behind Mike. It was early morning sun was just beginning to split the darkness of the night. It was cool and the ship moved slowly toward the land. The coast line shimmered with beauty but also set off some alarms in my head.

Mazatlan is a city in the Mexican State. We would soon be deep inside Mexico. Mazatlan has three large groups that settled this area. Spaniards and Indians in 1531, no surprise but the next largest immigrant group arrived from Germany. The Germans pushed Mazatlan into a thriving commercial seaport. Resort hotel's line the beaches and we had a reservation. I suppose I was just feeling a bit overwhelmed.

Again I had to let go of my anxieties; fear of the unknown, being in a strange land, not able to speak the language, ran freely over my thoughts. But right now, we joined all the people on deck and watched as the Mazatlan coastline came alive. Small boats sped past us, probably fishing early fishing boats. I could see silhouettes of the resorts cut right into the coast line.

The people around us started milling around and organizing their possessions for departure. They knew the routine; you could tell. I looked back at Mike and said, "Better get back to the room. Everyone's getting ready to leave."

Mike shook his head up and down and engaged in a slow trot back to the room. As we disembarked our eyes focused on a long line of people. They appeared to have been waiting all morning. They pulsated and seemed to go on forever.

"Is that the line to buy tickets?" I asked.

"Yes. We need to get into that line to buy a return ticket." Mike pointed out.

"It is a mile long!" I said. "It will take half the day!"

Mike raised his shoulders higher to try to see the end of the line. He was on his tip-toes when he exclaimed, "All right. We're not getting in that line. We don't have time. We not going to waste half a day on buying a one way ticket back." Mike lectured.

"So how are we going to get back?" I pointed out.

"No worries Nico. We are going to fly!" Mike laughed.

"Commercial?" I bellowed.

"Commercial!" Mike shot back. "I hope Mexicana Airlines has room for two more. I can make reservations at the hotel.

Mike was always one step ahead. I can't imagine how much this was costing him but money seemed to be no problem.

The Mazatlan coastline was beautiful but some parts were ragged and undeveloped. From our hotel, you could see other high rise resorts in either direction. We had a panoramic view of the water and were close enough to the shore to hear every wave break. It was great but Mike was having problems getting a flight back.

"La Paz is out." Mike frustratingly spit out. "Our only hope is San Jose de Cabo." It's closer to the plane; the only problem is we have to fly first class."

"How far is San Jose de Cabo from Cabo San Lucas?" I questioned, but catching on. "First class? Wow. I'm in."

Mike pointed out that it was about an hour from our plane. Our problem of transportation was solvable; just so we got a seat on the plane, and we had two days to explore Mazatlan. Mazatlan is below the Tropic of Cancer which puts it on the same latitude as Honolulu, Hawaii. I could feel the tropical heat and humidity through my senses; all of my pores were opening craving for some comfort. I needed to jump into some water and I headed down towards the beach in front of our hotel. Finally, the vacation part of our trip had manifested itself.

TAXI

The white wash of the small waves in front of our hotel made the beach area murky, creating poor visibility in the water. Snorkeling was out. However, the head high waves were fun to jump through. The day's heat had reached nearly 100 degrees and the humidity was off the charts. Needless to say, the water felt great.

My eyes looked upward at the parasailers sailing high overhead. It looked so fun and so scary at the same time. I would have no trouble giving it a try. Mike was looking into signing us up but the next few days were already booked. On top of that, it was really expensive. Mike was already forking out money for the flight back to San Jose Cabo. We also spent money on taxi's shuffling us around town. I actually welcomed the pace of our trip slowing down a bit. Up to this point, the trip had been a whirlwind of activity and adventure.

Mazatlan was mellow. We stayed close to the hotel and enjoyed the pools and beaches that our resort offered. For the first time, I didn't feel rushed.

The two days rejuvenated me. But the weather definitely was changing. The weather that greeted us with a clear, hot day when we arrived was now gray and overcast. A light rain dribbled down from the sky.

I started thinking about tomorrow. We were scheduled to

leave on Mexicana Airlines in the morning. The weather reports all posted a gray overcast, with light rain for two full days.

"Mike, no problem flying in the rain on a jet? Right?" I wanted some reassurance on the safety of flying in this weather.

"Oh. No problem. Those jets can fly in almost anything." Mike boasted.

"How hard would have to rain for these jets to have problems?" I nervously uncovered a hidden anxiety.

"Nick, you worry to much. We are going to make it back. All the way back. You can take that to the bank." Mike always tried to throw in humor. "Relax, and enjoy the ride!"

The rest of the day was uneventful. I started a book by Robin Cook, a medical suspense called Coma. I enjoyed the medical dramas. Theology books were always enjoyable too!

The rain forced us back in our room. Though I was deep into my book, I could hear the wind hurl and tiny droplets of rain hit our windows. The gutters were running and this storm was getting bigger by the minute.

I didn't sleep well at all. My senses would not let go of the sound the rain was making. Normally, I would love to hear the rain. It put me to sleep. Not tonight. I just wanted it to stop. It never did.

The morning came and we hustled to catch our taxi. We agreed to meet in front of our hotel for a ride to the airport. The gray clouds released a soft sprinkle of water. The wind was down and I was feeling better. Surely a jet could handle a light drizzle.

I saw the taxi and tried to wave him down but he drove right past me to pick up another couple down the way from us. I looked at Mike and then at my watch. We looked down the driveway and didn't see another taxi. Mike spoke first, "The next one; I'm sure the next one is ours!"

Fifteen minutes went by and so did five taxis two buses, and a food delivery truck. Our taxi was nowhere in sight. We were both frustrated and paced back and forth. "Call somebody. We're going to miss the plane!" I shouted.

Mike yelled, "Look, there he is!"

The taxi was green and dented on the side. It didn't have a sign on top but one on the side of the car. The driver was smiling and waving and hit the curb when he approached us. Mike and I vaulted back. He was twenty minutes late and almost ran us over.

He jumped out of the car, laughing and singing some song to himself. He said, "Mike Cross group? Hey, we be going to the airport."

"Yeah, that right." Mike responded, totally checking this guy out. "We're in a bit of a hurry!"

"No worries dude. Your flight will be behind. Everything in Mazatlan is slower. I will get you there." The driver said as he threw our baggage into the trunk.

I couldn't tell if this man was Mexican or Jamaican. His accent of Spanish/English and something else was interesting to say the least. He sure was happy. He never said he was sorry for being so late; acted as if nothing was wrong.

Everything became clear when we stepped inside the car. The smell hit my nostrils and penetrated my olfactory nerves. The aroma was intense. There was no mistake. That smell was marijuana! The good stuff! Before I could open my mouth the driver poured on the accelerator and raced into traffic. I turned and stared at Mike, "I guess I know why he was late."

Mike whispered, "What is that smell?"

Before I could answer, the driver belted out while laughing, "Ganga. Do you want to try some before your flight?"

Mike said, "What's ganja?"

I poked Mike in the ribs while the driver belly laughed and turned up the radio. "Mike, Ganga is marijuana."

"Oh!" Mike exclaimed trying to be cool. "No thanks, not this time."

"Maybe next time!" The driver came back. "This is the good ganga!"

Mike poked me back and whispered in my hear, "Are we okay?"

"Yeah. He's probably used to its effects. Seems like a happy guy" I whispered back.

I glanced down at the floorboard and noticed no carpet. I could see holes in the metal and actually see the ground. It was a thin layer of rusted metal that protected me and Mike's side was the same. In fact, the floor was completely wet; water from the puddles in the street had vaulted up into the car. Mike's feet were already dripping with water and more water was seeping in. Again the driver spoke, "Watch your feet. Sometimes it gets a little wet back there. Your luggage is fine. This rain shouldn't be here this time of year. I've been meaning to put carpet back down; that would help. Almost there."

"No problem," Mike blurted out. He was more concerned with how this guy was driving.

However, more water shot up from the road and through the holes. Once the smell of the ganga wore off the smell of mildew sprang forward. "This is ridiculous!" I looked straight at Mike.

Mike just smiled and shrugged his shoulders. "What's your name?" Mike questioned the driver.

"Jose." said the driver. I rolled my eyes.

"Do you know Carlos?" Mike was now playing with him. Jose just shook his head and pointed to the turnoff to the airport. We gave Jose a nice tip. Maybe he could fix his car. At least, our luggage was dry.

I was nervous about flying but I must have had a contact high from the pot because I just didn't care. However, the good luck that had followed us on the trip continued: two seats in first class.

We waited at the gate. The light rain still bothered me as I stared out the window. The tarmac and runway looked pretty wet. Other planes navigated the take-offs and landings without any problems so I figured we would be fine. I tried to relax.

Mike interrupted my solace. "Nick. I kinda wanted to try the ganga."

"You already did. How do you feel? I smiled.

"I didn't try any ganga. What do you mean? Mike said beginning to get emotional.

"The smoke in the taxi. You have a contact high. How do you feel? I asked again.

"I feel; feel; feel; relaxed. My God! Am I high?" Mike questioned.

"No. But probably just starting to feel the drug's effect. The taxi was hot boxed."

"Hot boxed? Mike continued, "The smoke. The drug is in the smoke."

"Yeah. You're right. Just a small hit of THC. The active chemical in pot. What do you think?" I was probing.

"I can see why people might like it. Maybe when we get back you could set up a chance for me to really give it a try." Mike explained.

"No problem. When we get back. Mike is smoking pot a sin?" I looked right at him.

"I don't know. Is drinking brandy? He shot back at me.

"Maybe. It depends if you get addicted to it. Addiction sucks.

Plus, the high could become your God. Anything that takes you away from God is potentially destructive." I was on a roll.

"Nico, you're a wise young man." Mike patted me on the back.

I couldn't judge anybody. I grew up around chain smoking, alcoholic, dysfunctional people. Many were in my family. I still loved them. My mother taught me not to label or judge people. No one knew what was in their heart. No one knew what they were going through. Everyone's reality was different. Mental health was ambiguous, she would teach me.

"God will judge you exactly the way you judged others", mom would say.

I thought that was prophetic. Right on. She went on to point out that we all had some good inside of us. "The Lord doesn't make junk." she would deadpan.

The drunk, addict, smoker, certainly would be challenged in their lives. No doubt. But also, sometimes, were the nicest people I ever met. My mom showed me sober people who were complete assholes and spiritually dead. Then she would point out drunks who were completely delightful. When Jesus said prostitutes and thieves would enter the kingdom before you he also meant drunks, addicts and various other sinners. He was talking to the most pure and righteous priest of the day. This teaching really resonated with me.

My mother would surround herself with dysfunctional personalities and try to squeeze the goodness out of them. She could relate to them, she was one of them. She had plenty of struggles. Relationships, alcohol, nicotine addiction, and family squabbles. She would try to hide all of them from me. However, I also saw her give up alcohol and nicotine; her hardest addictions. She gave money away and food to the church. She, true to herself, never gave up trying to become better.

I certainly learned we were responsible for ourselves sober or high. One sin couldn't produce damnation; likewise one good act wouldn't manifest salvation. We would be judged on the whole package; according to my own preconceived judgment.

I decided not to judge. It was too dangerous for me. It seemed the only logical way to live. Just because a small part of the apple was damaged, it didn't mean it couldn't be the sweetest apple in the bunch.

Father Mike seemed to embrace forgiveness and affirm goodness. He told me that he had a deep empathy for people. He could feel their pain. His priesthood would be about helping people.

Just like Jose predicted the flight was running late. We settled into the chairs at the gate and proceeded to read the news of the day. I needed to catch up on sports and my beloved San Francisco Giants. I had to see where they were in the standings. Still in third place behind the dreaded Dodgers. The giants still had September to catch them. Finally, forty five minutes later, we boarded.

The plane took off without a problem and soon we were flying above the clouds. It was only a two hour flight to San Jose de Cabo. We had a long day of travel in front of us. The rest of our flights would all be headed home.

I did feel much safer in the small jet than Mike's tiny plane. I shut my eyes and dreamed about getting home. I was starting to feel homesick. It always happened to me on vacations.

About eight days into the vacation I started feeling homesick. I must have a homing beacon that sounded an alarm at eight days. All my thoughts now turned to getting home. For now, I was content; from now on every flight would get me closer to home. It was a comforting thought.

HOMEWARD BOUND

We landed in San Jose del Cabo and hustled to the baggage check; a challenging day confronted us. We had to make it back to La Paz, with the plane and with enough time to find a hotel to stay overnight. It was already two in the afternoon and we had a one hour ride back to Cabo San Lucas and our plane. We had to untie the plane, prep for take-off and get clearance to actually launch the plane. That figured out to about 30 minutes. A fifty minute flight back to La Paz would get us in close to five o'clock. Plenty of time to find lodging; but enough variables to make us nervous.

"Mike. Can't we just stay in Cabo tonight and fly tomorrow morning?" I was searching for an easier path than Mike charted.

"We can do this Nico. We can be in La Paz by 6 pm at the latest. Plus, I'm itching to fly the plane. We'll be back at the Hotel Sol/Mar by 7." Mike proudly delivered. "Besides. And I hate to say this but, this starts our trip home. Every flight will draw us nearer and nearer to home. I'll have you home and sleeping in your own bed in three days." Mike's eyes widened as he finished.

"Three days? Who are you, Jesus Christ?" I joked.

"Yeah, probably three. I'm not Jesus. It will only take two days from La Paz if we get some good weather." Mike smiled and held up two fingers.

The formula for calming my homesick anxieties was hearing three days. I could handle three if I had to. Two days from La Paz. Music to my ears.

The taxi ride to the plane was smooth. No smell of ganga and a fully carpeted floorboard in the back seat. It took almost forty-five minutes to untie the plane. The knots in the rope made our task harder. At times we had to just cut the rope.

Finally, we got clearance to take-off and headed out for take-off. I couldn't believe the difference between the jet and our prop plane. I felt every bump, every vibration, every wind current in this plane. I heard the noise of the engine and the spinning of the rotor.

Once I accepted my environment I calmed down and relaxed. Still the differences between the planes were undeniable. Sitting in first class; on a 737 jet, my feet outstretched, being waited on and smothered in comfort. Falling asleep was easy. I could never fall asleep on Mike's Piper Cherokee. It was so cramped, I felt I was in the back seat of a Volkswagon Bug. I could not stretch my feet forward and they would continually cramp up and force me into a new position.

However, the view was panoramic. I could see everything and I think this is what I loved most. I flew over beautiful bays and some of Baja's finest beaches. It was worth it. Baja's real beauty was the coastline and beaches. The interior was flat and rather boring.

I watched Mike get back into his pilot mode; he was like a little kid. He loved to fly; no doubt, it was in his blood. The flight seemed short; we must have caught some good tailwinds.

We were on the ground and back in La Paz before 6. Shortly after landing Mike called the Hotel Sol/Mar. We lucked out. They had one room left for the night. Lady Luck had been with us for almost the entire vacation. God's grace stood in front of us and we seemed to get everything we needed. I was slowly starting to understand God's grace. Grace was energy. At least, a type of energy. That's how I perceived it. It made you feel good and realize that you're not alone.

The meal that evening, salmon, carna asada, with rice and beans melted into my mouth. Mike and I enjoyed our last dinner in Baja. Our conversation raced back over the events of the past week. Mike downplayed everything. We argued over how much the plane fish-tailed on the landing in San Felipe. Mike called it a slight back and forth event. I reminded him that the plane was pointing in the direction we landed; we had spun, a half circle!

Mike shook his head and replied, "Maybe at the end, the sand got pretty thick!"

"You lost control of the plane!" I shot back.

"No, not in San Felipe." Mike confidently said.

"Oh, you wanted the plane to spin." I said, we were both being silly.

Of course, Mike, true to form, didn't drink. I, on the other hand, drank freely. The evening had a happy hue. God's grace engulfed us and lifted our spirits. However, it was time to be homeward bound. However, we never realized just how much luck we would need to make it back home. The luck would border on miracle. We had no idea.

CATAVINA

We felt the deja vu of being back at the Hotel Sol/Mar. We lodged but one room away from our old room. I was starting to think about home; my friends and especially my girlfriend. We hustled a late dinner and relaxed in our rooms.

Mike had a map unwrapped and spread across our kitchen table. He was plotting our way home. Ever since our schedule changed he had been trying to find the quickest way home. He was deep in thought. I figured it was simple; retrace our route down to Cabo. Mike had other ideas, "Nick. I think we'll just skip San Felipe all together. Let's fly past San Felipe and get gas in Catavina. It has a landing strip and we should be able to refuel. We take-off, land a few hours later in Mexicali; go through customs and continue on to San Luis Obispo. We spend the night with my friends and have a short trip home to Watsonville. Two days! I'll have you home in two days!"

"Mike that sounds like a lot of flying. Can we do it?" I wondered.

"We can!" Mike smiled.

"When do we start?" I was excited, a chance to be home in my own bed in two days. It sounded great.

Mike preceded to tell me that we would need to be in the air by 7 tomorrow morning. We ate an early dinner and planned on getting some sleep but started reminiscing about our trip so far. Needless, to say it lasted late into the night.

I drank a couple of strong Margaritas; Mike, true to his word, didn't drink; Mike doesn't drink on the day before he flies. We figured it would be a smooth ride home, those thoughts would soon be exposed as erroneous.

We somehow managed to get into the air by 7am. The takeoff was smooth and the plane encountered little resistance from the calm morning air. I was relieved we would be skipping San Felipe. Our first landing and takeoff from that dirty sandy field was so intense. Catavina had to be better. It didn't take long to find out.

Mike signaled that we were getting close to Catavina's airport. I pressed the binoculars tight against my eyes. I looked forward and saw a long runway; dirt with no pavement. I could see two planes on the ground but no buildings. I had instant anxiety. We had been in this position before.

I spoke up, "Mike, is this the right place?"

"Yes, I believe so," Mike shot back. "Yes, look, two planes are on the ground. I'll do a fly by."

Catavina had to be the flattest piece of earth on the planet. The runway looked packed and long and no telephone wires were anywhere in site. I glanced at Mike who was enjoying these little challenges; landing on dirt runways.

"No pavement again," I breathed heavy.

"Nico, no problem. I see a car speeding toward the runway; I bet it's our fuel."

I looked at Mike. He looked strong and confident. I had learned that he felt good when he called me Nico. My anxiety had leveled out but I always was a little more alert during the landings.

Mike gave me the thumbs up and pointed the plane straight

down the landing strip. I learned from Mike that a landing was just a controlled fall from the sky. We were falling; but Mike was in control. Mike started letting the plane fall and we headed for touch down. The runway was packed and hard; Mike greased the landing. Very smooth.

We taxied back toward the two planes sitting on the ground. We saw children running out from behind the planes to great us. We stared at each other. This is exactly how it started in San Felipe. The children. I reached into my pocket and found three dollars.

Mike said, "Nico, welcome to Catavina. Our welcoming committee is back."

CARLOS

I pulled the last dollar out of my pocket and handed it to Maria, a cute girl with a smile that didn't stop. She spoke enough English to tell me her name and the names of her buddies. Deja vu invaded all my thoughts.

I asked Mike, "This is exactly what happened in San Felipe. The dirt runway, the children, no buildings, and no fuel. How long before Carlos drives up with our gas?"

Mike looked off in the distance. An old truck was indeed barreling towards us at a high rate of speed. Deja vu filled the air as Mike and I stared at each other.

"Mike, you don't really think it could be." My voice gave out mid-sentence.

"Oh my God Mike, it's Carlos!" I shouted.

"No way!" Mike's eyes had not yet put the truck with the man. "Yea, same truck, but it's got to be a different guy! We're two hours from San Felipe."

The truck came to a skidding stop just in front of the plane. A dust cloud choked everyone's windpipe for a few seconds and made the visibility blurred. A fog made of dust made it hard for my eyes to identify the man as he climbed out of the truck.

I massaged my eyelids to clear my vision. I looked directly at the man and saw him spit a large tobacco stained saliva stream right at our feet. He smiled and nodded his head up and down. "Necesitan gasolina?"

Silence. We were in psychogenic shock. What were the odds? It was Carlos.

Mike spoke first, "Speak English. We know you can, Carlos!" Mike was a little rude.

Carlos looked closely at us like he was surveying a map. He patted Mike on the back and said, "People are looking for you."

"What people?" I jumped in.

"The authorities!" Carlos proclaimed.

"What do you mean?" Mike shot back.

"Do you want fuel?" Carlos pointed to his truck.

I could still see the shotgun in the back of the truck. The same feelings I had back in San Felipe rushed back for a visit. I didn't trust this guy.

"Nick, they really think we're carrying drugs. They will be watching for us when we cross the border." Mike was feeling uneasy.

"Mike. We don't have anything but fish, my guitar and our clothes. What's the bother?"

Mike stared back at Carlos. What a stoic man. Just doing his job. "Nick, Carlos knows what's going on. Que pasa, Carlos?"

Carlos spat a wad of saliva drenched in tobacco juice just in front of us. He grinned and felt some of the chew juice drip down onto his chin. He wiped his chin and spoke, "All I know is I deliver fuel between here and San Felipe. I ask no questions; these men have guns. I get paid in cash. Just be careful when you reach Mexicali. I would stop in Loretto and ditch anything that might be considered contraband."

"Be careful?" I jumped in. "Mike's what's that about?"

Mike gazed out toward the flat desert and massaged his forehead. He spoke, "They could detain us; take the plane apart.

It could get nasty. They trust no one. Sometimes they keep the drugs they find. No rules, ethics, or morality here. Carlos is right. We have to fly right through this gauntlet. We've done nothing wrong. Nick can you believe it? All this because we landed at the wrong place?"

I shook my head and said, "We'll be okay Carlos, filler up."

Mike pulled me over away from Carlos and whispered, "Nico, no worries. We both start praying right now for safe passage. Meditate on the words 'safe passage.' We'll be all right; safe passage."

I immediately started chanting "safe passage" I could sense that Mike was concerned and searching for more answers. Mike's faith was so strong. That's where he started solving all his problems. He was definitely connected to God's divine nature. He believed he could figure his way out of anything.

I shook my head and told Mike to get the camera. I wanted a picture of Carlos, the truck and the kids. We took no pictures in San Felipe and now we had a second chance.

Carlos only posed once when I moved over toward him while he was pumping the fuel. I couldn't help thinking of what tribulations were still in our path. We said our goodbyes to the children and to Carlos. He turned out to be a nice man. Before Carlos left, he grabbed both of us and wished us luck. He also said, "Remember. Loretto primero; first. Check the plane make sure everything is okay. Then fly to Mexicali. Remember."

Mike shut the door and said, "What's he talking about? We can make it all the way to Mexicali; easy. It doesn't make sense!"

"Maybe we get jumped in Loretto? Maybe he's setting us up!" I surmised.

"You do realize if we stop in Loretto we would have hit every major city in Baja?" Mike continued to name them all,

"Mexicali, Loretto, Catavina, La Paz, Cabo San Lucas and San Jose del Cabo. Plus Loretto could be our bathroom break."

"Mike did you hear me? He could be setting us up!" My voice was serious.

"I know Nick. No one is out to get us. They couldn't possibly know when we'd be here. Carlos was giving us a warning. A sign. A puzzle. Why? He knows we could make it to Mexicali. Search the plane? Why?"

Mike had finished a smooth take off and climbed up to five thousand feet. Very smooth flying. We both talked about the strange request Carlos gave us. Land in Loretto? Why? Search the plane. Why? Did a ghost put drugs on our plane during the flight?

I finally had some clarity. "Mike, our only problem is landing at the wrong field at the wrong time. Mike, how do druggies transport their drugs from country to country?"

Mike quickly answered, "Planes, boats, stuffed animals, toys. Anything that doesn't draw attention to itself."

"What about a priest and a friend flying on vacation?" I thought out loud.

"What do you mean?" Mike's eye's widened as he looked right at me.

"Mike someone planted something in or on our plane!" I shouted.

"No one has had access to our plane. I checked everything. We're carrying nothing but what we put on the plane." Mike argued.

"Mike I think we put it on the plane. Like you said, these guys are good. We didn't even know it." I started looking all over the plane.

"Nick, if you're right Carlos could have just saved our lives!"

Mike frantically looked all around the plane. Both of us

searched everything we could touch. Our fish, the guitar and bags were in the back; we couldn't get to them until we landed. Mike's usually smooth flying was erratic and stressed. We continued looking at places we already looked.

Mike felt his seat and spoke out, "I feel totally spooked about this. If we land in Loretto there could be drug runners waiting for us. If we don't, we might be carrying drugs directly into Mexicali and the customs agents. Nick, it's time to pray. Lord Jesus, help us."

Mike was spooked. He always swallows when he's nervous and we was gulping down mountains of air. It all seemed impossible. Maybe just a misunderstanding. I looked at Mike and said, "Land in Loretto. I have to go to the bathroom."

Mike looked at me and smiled. He sat up in his chair nodded his head. "Nico, Loretto it is."

I knew he wanted to land there just to say he landed at every town in Baja. He started whistling and settling into a comfortable position. In one hour we would be in Loretto. I kept looking around the plane. What did we miss?

LORETTO

Mike flew over the Loretto airfield twice. We didn't even know what we were searching for. Two planes, were below us, a nice runway, dirt of course, but it looked packed and hard. Mike gave me a thumbs up and positioned the plane for final approach.

I continued to look for anything that looked odd. I saw an access road that led away from the runway and seemed to go on forever. However, no cars. This was in the middle of nowhere; perfect for drug runners.

I felt uneasy, full of fear. I also realized we could be making this whole ordeal up. A huge misunderstanding. Still some things didn't make sense. Carlos' warning. Drugs. How could we be caught up in all of that? "Okay, Mike, did Carlos set us up or put drugs on our plane?"

Mike suggested, "We landed in three other cities since we first saw him. Let's land and thoroughly search the plane. This place looks safe enough. We need to figure out our next move."

The landing was rather rough, unusual for Mike. We bounced twice before the wheels settled into a smooth roll. Mike taxied the plane to the far end of the runway and pointed in position for take-off. No reason to go anywhere near those planes. We got out and surveyed the flat landscape. No people or sounds.

"Okay. Let's get everything off the plane and search."

Mike raced to unlock the cargo hold. Mike fished for the key on his key chain and nervously jiggled the key into the keyhole. He quickly grabbed my guitar and handed to me. He then grabbed the styrofoam boxes that held the fish. They were heavy as I placed them on the ground.

Mike finished by throwing our suit cases next to the fish. He looked deep into the rest of the compartment. He looked at me and said, "Nothing. That's it. That's all we have. Look through everything! Think like a drug runner; where would he hide the stuff?" Mike lectured.

"On your plane!" I said half jokingly.

After fifteen minutes of an extensive search we found nothing. We looked back in the plane itself. We touched all the seat cushions: no tears or bumps. Mike even looked in the engine itself. Nothing. We were getting frustrated and more confused.

We started putting everything back on the plane when Mike exclaimed, "Well that's it. The plane is clean! Let's see what happens in Mexicali. This place gives me the creeps. Let's get out of here."

"Mike, think. What's the only thing that was put on the plane by someone else other than us?" I wasn't giving up.

Mike responded. "We've gone over that. The fish. But you searched the fish. I'm sorry to say we can't eat them now. We broke the seal; they will spoil before we get home."

"It has to be the fish!" I shot back.

"Okay. Get them out of the plane. Let's search them again." Mike rolled his eyes as he spoke.

We each grabbed a box and opened them carefully and slowly. It was as if we were defusing a bomb. I opened my box again and grabbed first part of the fish. I saw the head and about 1/3 of the body. Mike glanced in and picked it up. It was my Dorado. No doubt about that. It looked normal; nothing unusual.

Mike spoke urgently, "Turn it over."

I said, "Well we definitely can't eat them now!"

"Turn it over!" Mike's voice was serious.

I slowly turned the dorado over and saw an incision down the belly of the fish. The slice was from the bottom of the mouth to it's midsection. However, it looked like a surgeon had sutured it shut. Odd.

I questioned Mike, "Why would they start to fillet the fish and then suture it shut? Mike, get a knife!"

Mike hustled around the plane and retrieved from the pilot's seat his lucky Swiss army knife and ran back to me.

I was staring at the stitches. They were sewn tight; you had to look close to see them; cut perfectly too. I lost my patience waiting for Mike and starting putting pressure on the incision. I popped the first stitch when Mike yelled, "No Nick. Stop! Do not tear them open."

He stopped me just in time.

"Mike I can easily tear it open." I looked right at him.

"We can't damage what's inside. We don't know what we're up against." Mike said while he opened the knife and carefully cut away a couple of stitches.

It was like I was watching a surgeon. Finally Mike cut the final ten all at once and opened up the fish completely.

What our eyes saw put us both into shock. Our legs buckled as we watched fifteen small packets fall to the ground. The packets were filled with a white powder. They all hit the ground but didn't open. No damage.

"Cocaine!" I yelled. "Oh my God. What have we gotten into?"

Mike stared at the white packets and said, "I bet we find more in the rest of the fish."

We gutted the rest of the fish and found forty five packets in all. No wonder the fish were so heavy. "How much is here?" Mike asked.

"I don't know but I'd say 10 to 15 pounds of very pure cocaine." I countered.

"Dear Jesus, help us!" Mike said as he knelt down to pray and think. "I am so sorry for getting you into this. I never dreamed, not in a million years this could happen."

I knelt beside him and patted him on the back. "We're in deep. They used us and we didn't even know it!

"Do you know what this means, Nick?" Mike calmly asked.

"We're drug runners." I tried to joke.

"Yeah. And something else. Someone is waiting for us to deliver the coke. They are waiting for us. They have probably been following us." Mike was probably right.

I jumped back in "But where?"

Mike talked fast, "Mexicali? Calexico? Watsonville?"

"That doesn't make sense. They don't know our flight plans back in California." I stated.

"You're right." Mike came back. "There is only only one place that they know where we will be. Customs. We have to go through customs in Mexicali."

"But couldn't we go through customs somewhere else?" I was reaching. "How could they know?" Who have you told our flight plans too?"

"The bartender in San Felipe. I had two margaritas." Mike was thinking out loud, "We talked about Carlos, and I told him our itinerary. The bartender."

"I thought you said he was cool. The bartender, Carlos, the

hotel Sol/Mar and their staff. They're all in on it. Unreal." I thought I had figured it out.

"Nice deduction. You're probably right. So it's going to happen in Mexicali; they're waiting for us." Mike looked at the cocaine. If we're caught with this we might not get home for a very long time. What are we going to do with this? "Mike clutched a small baggie of coke.

I glanced at the cocaine in amazement. They got a lot of it into a little space. I figured since these druggies were so sophisticated we would have to be even smarter to get out of this. I looked at Mike and said, "Well now that we have discovered it, we can't fly with it; it's illegal!"

"Yes, but if we don't deliver the goods, our lives could be in danger. Again, I'm so sorry for getting you into this." Mike pointed out.

"Our lives our already in danger, Mike. Some bad people are waiting for their cocaine. They would probably kill us for it. What's our plan? We have to have a plan!" I breathed heavily and looked at Mike.

Silence.

I didn't feel safe in Loretto, Mexicali, or anywhere in Baja. At this very moment, we had two choices: both could get us killed. One, place the cocaine back into the fish, wrap the lid tight, and hope the people who owned it would, at some point, just take it. Second, land in Mexicali, alert the federales and hand over the coke. These options presented considerable risk: jail, fines, or even death!

We searched for a third alternative but it would not manifest itself. We prayed for ideas, a plan, any path that could get us safely out of the country. Mike looked at me and said, "You know, Carlos probably saved our lives!"

I countered, "How?"

111

"If he didn't ask us to land in Loretto we wouldn't know any of this. If we flew straight into customs with this stuff we would be in a Mexican jail for a long time." Mike explained.

I still wondered, "How did he know? What did he know? Who did he know?" my mouth was just running off, "He lives here. He looks out for himself. Maybe because you're a priest! He's a Catholic; you're a Catholic priest caught in a trap. Everyone's Catholic down here. He did save us; or you."

Mike, looked me in the eye and said, "Nico, you used to hate this guy! But you might be right."

"Mike you're attached to God. He can't send you into a place you might die. Being tied to a priest killing for drug runners; isn't that a mortal sin?" I joked.

I could tell by Mike's expression he didn't think I was funny. He said, "I kinda liked that guy. I really believe he is our guardian angel. At least we have a chance now. God is helping us; we just have to be smart." Mike winked, and continued, "I do have a plan."

"A plan." I repeated, "Let's hear it."

I excitedly moved closer to Mike. He started talking, "First of all, you're right. We leave the cocaine here. I do not want to fly with it on my plane. We bury it; carefully not to break any container. We cover it with rocks. That stuff is our ticket home!"

I liked this part and wanted to support Mike. "Mike, this will give us leverage. We have to be careful burying the coke. The rocks, maybe at the end of the runway, can act as a headstone. Anyone could find it, yet no one would know it's there, except for us."

Mike continued my thoughts, "The rocks will protect the coke from the desert heat and direct sunlight. Then will fly to Mexicali, play dumb, have nothing illegal on the plane and hopefully head home."

Mike had one flaw in his plan. The people who own this cocaine were waiting for it. They would detain us at some point and take the fish. I questioned, "Mike, what happens when they find that the coke is gone?"

Silence. Mike put his hand on his forehead and gave himself a five second massage. "I guess that where it could get complicated."

"Mike you forget our leverage." I shot back. "We know where it is; they don't. They need us. It's a simple deal. We will tell them where the drugs are; they give us safe passage home."

"I get it. One step at a time. Play dumb; maybe they take the fish and off we go. Search the fish, we come clean and make the deal. We have to be cool and ready for anything. Again, Nico, I'm so sorry for getting you into this. Your mom is going to kill me!"

We hurriedly, yet gently buried the cocaine on the far end of the runway on the right side. It stood out yet blended into the landscape perfectly. First, we carefully took all the coke out of the fish. I put the fish back into the styrofoam box and sealed it with duct tape. I put it back on the plane. Second, we dug a small hole, placing the coke gently inside, and covered the top with rocks. It almost resembled a small western tombstone. The rocks didn't seem out of place, we were both comfortable the coke was protected from the sun. Certainly this place didn't get many visitors.

We could be in Mexicali in less than an hour. Mike punched up the planes power and soared into the air. We flew, drug free, for the first time in three flights.

My thoughts turned to Carlos. Surely, he was one of them, yet he tried to help us. He knew they would try to use us. He warned us without giving anything away. I hoped the bad guys wouldn't figure out that he helped us; or stole the drugs for himself.

We were flying right into the heart of danger; we had no choice. The question was where were they hiding? These drug runners managed to be invisible to us up until this point. I'm sure they would like to stay invisible. All we could do was pray and rehearse every scenario we could think of. To survive, we needed to turn into actors. We had to muster courage, bravery and coolness.

The hour long flight seemed to pass in minutes. Mike started his descent into Mexicali and asked for clearance to land. My shirt was completely drenched. So much for staying cool.

FATHER ADAMS

Mike's erratic landing betrayed his anxiety level. Three bounces before the wheels could grab and roll. His stress was understandable. Our lives; our very futures were now in jeopardy.

We watched every plane we passed. At any moment someone would jump out and detain us; but from where, when, and who, were the unknowns.

Mike broke the silence, "Okay, you know the plan. Play dumb. We don't know anything. Just follow my lead."

"What lead?" I gasped.

"I'm throwing the whole Catholic church at them!" Mike shouted.

I looked straight into his eyes, "What does that mean?"

Suddenly, it all started to unfold. A police car headed out toward us. His lights were on and he as waving his arms to follow him. He forced us to turn the plane and headed us straight toward a hangar, just outside the terminal. The driver continued to wave his arms and motioned us to continue straight inside the hangar. This wasn't good. They were waiting for us.

Mike proceeded to park the plane and cut the power. Two more cars sped up to the plane and parked behind us. We weren't going anywhere. Mike reached in the back of the plane and grabbed a black shirt. He talked while he put it on, "I have to put on my Roman collar."

"Is this what you meant when you said you would throw the church at them?" I was confused.

"Follow my lead, you will understand. Mike reached for me and touched my forehead with him the palm of his hand. He said a prayer and finished with, "Help Nick get home."

Frantically Mike finished dressing. He was now dressed in black; though his shirt was completely wrinkled. His white collar in place, he looked like a priest. We blessed ourselves and climbed out of the plane.

Six policemen stood at attention close to their cars and one walked toward us He greeted us with a smile and warmly opened with, "Sorry to put you through this but we believe that this plane is carrying drugs. What are your names and why are you in Baja?"

Mike stepped forward, almost getting into the policeman's personal space. "Yes, I'm sorry too. I am Father Mike Cross and this is Father Adams; we're here on vacation. I can assure you, there are no drugs on my plane."

My brain had a brain freeze when he said Father Adams. Mike said it. I heard it. Now I am a priest? The policeman said, "I am captain Eber of the Mexican Police. Nice to meet you Father Cross and you too Father Adams." He looked right at me. "Pretty young for a priest, huh?" He stared at me, close enough for me to smell his breath.

"I went into the seminary when I was 17. I had an early vocation." I was sweating bullets as I talked.

"What order are you in Father Adams?" Captain Eber inched closer.

"I'm Jesuit. Founded in 1540 by St. Ignatius. Ignatius

encouraged Jesuits to share our insights with everyone. It's the basis of our spirituality." I tried to sound important.

Mike looked at me with amazement. "I am Jesuit too." He bellowed right back into Eber's face to get his attention off me.

Eber wrinkled his face and spit on the ground. "I like Franciscans. I am familiar with the Catholic faith. I am an educated man. Perhaps, Father, this is all a mistake. I hope so." Eber finished with a nice tone and added, "Please get your passports out. Father Cross; may we search your plane?"

"Yes, of course." Mike said as he stepped away from the plane. I followed his lead as we watched two men run past us to the plane. Eber wasn't through with us. "Father. Cross do you have a cargo hold?"

Mike signaled yes and pulled out his keys. He walked over to the plane and opened up the door. The boxes with the fish were in plan view. "Help yourself." Mike stepped away from the opening and motioned for someone to look inside. Two men, raced to the door and pulled out everything. The boxes, my guitar and our luggage.

The men talked in Spanish; Eber signaled them to take everything into a room that was adjacent to us. It looked like an office. The hangar had other rooms; it looked like some sort of command center. Eber stayed with us. He was the leader, no doubt. He said, "This will be over quickly."

Eber, Mike and I watched the men through the outside window. They seemed upset; one, raced out the door and sprinted up to Eber. He whispered in Eber's ear. They looked at each other and then back at us. They started another conversation in Spanish when Eber turned toward us with a most foul look on his face. "Father Cross. Their seems to be no drugs on your plane. But, we have a report that states that this plane had drugs on it. We know you landed at a known drug runway outside San Felipe."

Mike interrupted captain Eber, "We were lost. That was my fault. We didn't know where we were!"

"Shut up!" Eber pulled his gun out of his holster and pointed it at Mike's forehead. The other policeman pulled his gun as well and pointed it at me. I froze. I had never been so scared but I was also focused.

"Father Cross. I talk to you because you are older. What's going on? Where are the drugs?" Eber cocked his weapon.

Mike was incredibly calm. "No no no. We don't know anything about drugs. We do not know what you are talking about. We could never knowingly transport drugs on our plane. It is a sin! We have to be back in Watsonville, California, in two days to do a funeral. We were just on vacation."

Eber smiled. It seemed that he was enjoying himself. "Okay, Father. However, my superiors were told we would have a drug bust today. What am I going to tell them? We lost the drugs?" Eber slowly lowered his gun.

"Forgive me, Father. We are dealing with some bad guys. You know this job is hard. Catching the druggies, you know, they use all of us and we don't even know." Eber holstered his gun. He said, "Take them."

Captain Eber's men herded us into another room off the one we saw. As we walked through the door I could see the holding cell. Made of old fashioned bars and a swinging door it creaked as they shut us in. This was jail. They shoved us against the back wall. I could hear one man say in English, "Oh, sorry Father." It was a sarcastic remark and all his buddies laughed out loud. Another man leaned in and called me over. He said, "Father, will you hear my confession?"

He seemed sincere. He didn't want the others to hear our conversation. I whispered, "Sure, when this gets all sorted out." He looked at me and blessed himself. He was wearing a crucifix around his neck. He kissed the crucifix. The Catholic thing was starting to work. I would be dead right now I wasn't impersonating a priest. Mike's plan had kept us alive but now we were in jail.

We could see all of Eber's men huddled up around him. We could tell they were arguing over the next move. The good thing about being in jail is we were finally alone. We could talk freely. They left no one to watch us.

I spoke first, "Father Adams?"

Sorry, it was all I could think of. Hard to kill a priest, huh. It worked. Anyhow, I think this part of our plan is over. Phase Two is about to unfold. Remember, stay strong, don't back down."

We sat for thirty minutes before Eber came back. He didn't seem happy.

Captain Eber entered the room with authority and instantly created fear. I was hoping to uncover the God connection in him. The Spirit of God was in him. He was a Catholic, educated and knowledgeable about church history. He had faith, they all did, we just had to tap into their sense of humanity.

Mike thought that we could influence other people's actions by praying to their guardian angel. Systematic Theology. The belief in angels and devils. The church believed in all kinds of Angels. Mike went so far as to ask his congregation to pray to the guardian angel of our enemy or someone we were having a problem with. He said guardian angels can help us through life. Pray to them for a change of heart. Pray to them to instill faith, courage or forgiveness.

I glanced at Mike as Eber charged forward toward us. Mike was deep in prayer.

I whispered, "Guardian angel?"

"Mike opened his eyes and blinked, "I am way ahead of you."

Eber grabbed our arms and pushed us into a different room. One table. No windows. Four chairs and six ashtrays.

Eber asked us to sit and lit up a cigarette. He offered us a smoke; we both declined. He took a deep drag and sucked down as much nicotine as he could. He sat back and crossed his legs. "We have a problem! You see, my boss is not happy. He is on his way here to interrogate you. Yes, he wants a little chat with both of you. You see, he is not Catholic. If you don't tell him what he wants, he will hurt you. Neither I or my men will be able to protect you. He is upset that I couldn't get the job done."

"The job?" I asked.

"Torture!", Mike bellowed out. "Torture."

Eber took another hit off his cigarette and moved his head up and down. "You see, Father Cross and Father Adams, not one of my men would touch you. We do believe, at least, one of you is really a priest. We don't torture priests. However, priests are not normally drug runners." Eber smiled and stared at me. He continued, "Please Father Cross, my boss will be lethal. He has a lot at stake. Please, tell me where the drugs are!"

Mike jumped out of his seat, "We've told you the truth."

I almost blurted out the truth as Mike spoke. It seemed like the perfect time but Mike didn't think so. The boss scared me plenty. Eber stood up and pleaded, "I won't be able to protect you!"

"I know Eber," Mike stood. "Thanks for all you've done for

us. God bless you and your family. Mike finished with the sign of the cross and I mimicked his hand motions with my own.

Eber left the room and locked the door behind him. I had anxiety. "Mike this room is where bad things happen. No windows. Isolated away from the terminal. No one will hear us scream!"

"Nico, you watch too many movies." Mike verbally slapped me.

I instantly questioned Mike, "Why didn't we just tell Eber the truth? The hatchet man is coming. It could have all worked out. Why didn't you tell Eber?"

Mike moved closer to me and said, "They are trying to scare us. No one has touched us yet. In fact, they've treated us pretty well I think."

"Mike I had a gun, loaded and cocked, pointed at my forehead." I would say that was intense." I shot back.

"We bought more time. We will know when it's time to tell the truth. Pray that our guardian angels alert us when that time is here." Mike sat and tried to relax. Under the circumstances it gave us something to do. Besides, if anyone was spying on us we looked like priests who were praying. I prayed for no violence. Peace. My hands shook as the door slowly opened. I thought we might have more time. The boss sure got here fast.

Eber followed the boss along with two other men. He motioned for each man to stand on either side of us and hold our arms. The boss was tall and muscular; with biceps as large as my waistline. He had a trimmed beard and gold around his neck. He wore a tight T shirt to show off his trim upper body. His arms were laced with tattoos. I saw a pentagram, the mark of the devil on one arm and the virgin Mary on the other. Half his face was lathered in scar tissue. A mustache covered his upper lip and a light beard creased his face and neck.

How could this guy have a guardian angel? I feared my prayers were in vain.

He spoke with a raspy tone but clear English. "Where are the drugs?"

We were silent. The boss pulled out his knife; a twelve inch blade with serrated teeth. He smiled and open his eyes wide. He looked possessed with anger. "Last chance. Where are the drugs?"

Mike spoke but his voice was quivering. "We don't know."

"Really," The boss came back. "Well Father Cross. I hear you're the pilot. It's too bad pilots can't fly without hands!" The boss reached for Mike's arm and laid it across the table. The two men next to Mike pinned his arm down flat. The boss raised his knife and said, "I am gonna do it." He looked possessed.

"Stop! Enough!" I screamed at the top of my voice.

Instantly, the boss moved over to me. I couldn't move. Eber's men held me tight. I stared down the boss's weapon and watched him lay the knife directly across the carotid artery on my throat. I froze.

The boss spoke, "Stop. Why should I stop?"

I could feel the weight of the blade against my neck. I was petrified.

This time Mike screamed, "Don't hurt him. Let's make a deal."

The boss pulled the knife off me and pulled out a hand gun concealed in his pants. He pointed it at Mike's forehead and said, "A deal! Are you kidding me. I will kill both of you when this is over."

Mike boldly proclaimed, "Yeah, but you won't have the coke."

Eber joined in, "Father, how do you know the drug we're looking for is cocaine?"

"Because I know where it is. Buried somewhere in Baja." Mike was gaining stature.

The boss gave Eber a dirty look and grabbed Mike's head and pulled it close to his face, "I thought lying was a sin. Transporting drugs in our country is a major offense; certainly a sin.

I interrupted the boss, "We didn't know the drugs were in the fish. It was by accident that we found them. We are two priest on vacation. We can't fly with drugs, we buried them and moved on."

"Shut up! Everyone shut up," The boss fired his weapon into the air. The sound was deafening and brought silence to the room instantly. "Okay, Father. What is your deal?"

Eber knew the Boss was losing his patience and pleaded for Mike to talk. Mike proclaimed, "The deal is simple. We will tell you where the cocaine is. You let us go. We never see each other again."

The Boss took a step back, calmed himself down and asked Eber if we were really priests.

Eber said, "Yes, from Watsonville, California."

The Boss massaged his chin and got nose to nose with Mike, "Here's the deal Padre. You tell us where the coke is; we verify it, test it. If it's undamaged, clean and all there, you can leave. However, if something doesn't pan out. I will shoot you both and confiscate your plane. I could use another plane; I hear yours runs well."

The Boss turned toward Eber and shouted. "Now that wasn't so hard. Get the stuff!" as he bolted out of the room.

After the Boss cleared the door Eber raced over to us and pushed us back down into our chairs. He said, "I'm glad you're both alive. It doesn't always turn out this way. We have a lot to talk about."

ESCAPE

Mike proceeded to tell Eber everything we did. "We accidentally landed on a dirt runway we thought was San Felipe's airfield. It was my fault. We had a faulty map. However, the fish didn't go on the plane till La Paz. Who is part of this drug cartel? The fishermen? We gave the fish to them to clean and cut. The Hotel Kitchen staff put the fish on dry ice and sealed the boxes." Mike tried to answer his own question. "It had to be the kitchen staff."

Eber looked at Mike, winced and talked quickly, "Father do not be concerned about such matters; we will talk to them all. We will catch them; be sure of that. I only want you to tell me where the cocaine is. Where is the cocaine, Father Cross?"

Mike sighed, looked at me and told Eber exactly where we hid the coke. He retraced every footstep we took in La Paz; he talked to Eber but I don't think he trusted him. We tried to figure out who the criminals were. Mike just rambled on, "I think you should contact that fishing boat. They took our fish and gave it to the hotel. Come to think of it, they were very unprofessional; getting drunk when we snorkeled. Right Nick?"

Before I could speak Eber jumped in, "But the Kitchen crew put the fish into the boxes. They sealed them. It's always the last person to touch the good's."

Mike, not to be out done came back, "Yes, but who could

suture the fish so tight. You hardly noticed them. I think fisherman."

Eber finished, "It's probably both groups. The fishermen load the drugs, suture the fish, and hand it off to the hotel. The hotel seals it and gives it back to the tourist. You fly it out of the country for them and they pick it up somewhere along the line. Clean, invisible getaway. Now we have some firm leads. Thank you Father."

I had to say something, "Okay. How do they know where we will be at any given time?"

Eber answered, "They are following you."

"All the way home? How do they know our itinerary?" I had many questions.

Eber come over the top, "Leave that up to us. It's our job." Eber raised and walked out of the room. He had two guards stay with us; they both nearly genuflected and took their positions. Everyone wanted this to be over soon.

Eber quickly returned with two more guards. He walked straight up to Father Cross and asked him if he was ready.

"Ready for what?" Mike responded. "I told you everything I know."

"I know Father. Gracias. Now we need you to fly two of my men to the drugs." Eber stared at Father Cross.

"That wasn't part of the plan!" Mike shouted out. "In my plane?"

"Why of course. Your plane. The boss insisted that we use your plane. He also wanted you to be the pilot. Adams, I mean Father Adams, stays here." Eber motioned to me.

"No deal. Fr. Adams and me stay together." Mike grabbed my arm.

Eber took out his gun and pointed at my head. Mike yelled, "No guns."

Eber, holstered his weapon. Two guards were on one side of us and two on the other. Eber, spoke, "Sorry. The boss wants Adams here; it will be good motivation for you to get the drugs. If you don't come back with the drugs; Adams is dead. Of course you would be too!"

"Of course." Father Cross positioned his body closer to Eber. He could nearly look down his nostril when he said, "Eber, I will be back with drugs; are we free to go after that; or should we expect more?"

"The boss said I could set you free." Eber answered.

"Swear on it, Eber." Mike wasn't playing games.

"I give you my word, Father." Eber softly returned.

"I need fuel. No guns! Two of your guys should be able to take care of me." Mike was giving the orders.

"Father Mike you will have a gun to your head the entire flight; both ways. If you make it back. I hope so Father. I hope so."

As the conversation ended, two of the guards closest to me pulled me toward the cell. Father Cross yelled at me, "We will be in San Luis Obispo by nine o'clock. This will be over soon. Hang in there. Just give us a couple of hours." Mike looked around the room and finished so everyone could hear, "Anyone hurts Father Adams is going straight to Hell!"

Eber grabbed Mike and herded him toward the plane. I watched out the window as Mike and two guards got into the Archer II. I could see that fuel was being added and they cleaned the windshield. The plane started beautifully. Mike waved to me and started slowly heading out. I gave him a big thumbs up. However, I couldn't help notice the man squeezed into the space behind Father Cross was a guard with a gun to Mike's head. This would be Mike's most stressful flight yet.

I started praying but soon was distracted by questions in my head. Why didn't they use their own plane? Surely, the police had a helicopter. Radios communication, other departments. Being separated from Mike scared me. My thoughts were interrupted by Eber opening my cell and pulling up a chair. He saw how frightened I appeared and said, "Now we will find out the truth."

"I am worried about Father Cross." I spoke the truth.

Eber didn't hesitate, "Or maybe this is all a lie. A charade. We will know soon enough."

"Are you really going to let us go?" I nervously asked.

"That was the deal. However, everything has to fall into place." Eber finished.

"You will get the drugs. You will have your drug bust, you can count on that. Maybe you will get a promotion." I was terrible at jokes.

Eber just smiled and said, "Father Adams, I don't need a promotion."

Thirty minutes had gone by since Eber left the room; it gave me some time to reflect on what we went through. I listened to Eber's and Mike's whole conversation and I never heard one word about Carlos. Carlos was the reason we landed in Loretto. Mike told Eber we both had to go the bathroom and he needed to land the plane in our interrogation. Carlos had some part in all this but I couldn't piece it together. One thing I did know, Mike was smart not to give Carlos away. If Eber, or the Boss, found out that Carlos helped us, his life would be in danger.

Every passing minute made me more uncomfortble I was pacing back and forth. I noticed one of the men motioned me over to him. I headed to him and asked, "Is everything okay?"

The guard, just a very young man, almost a boy, returned, "Father Adams, I must ask a favor from you."

Before I could answer, the telephone rang in the room

outside out own. We raced to the door with the guards. Eber, patiently walked to the phone and picked it up. He didn't say one word. He just listened. His eyes stretched as he turned and looked at us. He hung up the phone and walked towards me, arms open wide. He wrapped his arms around me. "Father, we have the drugs. You are free to go."

The whole room erupted into spanish joy. The man who wanted to talk to me grabbed me and said, "You can go home, Father Adams. You can go home!"

Father Cross still wasn't home and we certainly were not together. Now we would find out if they really meant their side of the deal. I tried to imagine what Father Mike had been through. I hurriedly ran out of the hangar to watch for Mike's plane. My heart pounded through my chest and my breathing was deep and steady. I watched ten planes land and then the Archer II came screaming in. The happiness I felt when Mike landed and taxied back to our hanger. We all rushed out to meet him.

We hugged, and Mike said, "Wow. You okay?"

"Yes" I replied.

The love fest lasted a few more moments and Mike hustled me toward the plane. "Nico, if we take off now, I can get us to San Luis Obispo. We have to fly at night, I'm instrument trained for night flying. Are you okay with that?"

"That sounds heavenly Father," I jumped back to Father Adams.

We loaded our suitcases back on board the plane. The fish, already rotten by exposure and my guitar; smashed to pieces, would stay in Mexicali. We checked our camera's and everything we could touch in the cockpit. Nothing had been touched. Odd, I thought. Wouldn't they want to check the inside of the plane?

Out of the corner of my eye I saw Eber walking out of his office and toward the plane. His men followed him out. He called out as he walked, "Father Cross, Father Adams. I am sorry for all of this. I am happy by the way things worked out. We have filled your plane with fuel. Compliments of my men." He turned and pointed towards them. "Father Cross, Father Adams, we have one more request of you."

Mike walked toward Eber, "Of course, Eber. Anything."

"Would you be kind enough to give us a blessing." Eber asked, "And the boy wants to go to confession with Father Adams."

Mike fumbled over his search for words. I was stunned, unable to talk. Mike tried to make a comeback, "Eber, yes, I mean of course, no problem. Hey, Father Adams can do the blessing and I will hear the boy's confession". What's his name?"

Eber looked directly at me and said, "Manuel. His name is Manuel and he wants Father Adams. Any problems Father Cross?"

Mike was rattled but said, "Of course not! Just thought you'd want the old man for confession."

I went over to Manuel and told him to go to the back of the plane and wait for me. I told him I had to get ready but would be with him shortly. I walked to the front of the plane and signaled for Mike to join me. When no one could hear I whispered, "Am I going to Hell because I do a fake confession?"

"Shuush...be quiet." Mike put his hands over my mouth. He glared at me and said, "You know what to do. I will absolve him of his sins through you. Remember, the sign of the cross at the end. He's just a young boy. Probably gonna tell you he masturbated. When you're done, we bless them, give some hugs and get the hell of out here. Comprende?"

Mike had his hand on his mouth the entire time. I slowly

walked to the tail section of the plane. Manuel was pacing back and forth. He had a rosary in one hand and a cigarette in the other.

Once my eyes surveyed Manuel's stress level, my mind journeyed back to my last experience of confession. It had been a long time; maybe two, three years. I couldn't remember the time or place. Catholics, though encouraged to attend the sacrament of confession once a year, or when in serious sin, didn't jump at the chance to go to the sacrament. In fact, probably only 50% went once a year. I was one of those. I didn't mind telling God my sins in my prayers. He certainly knew all of them.

The church's response to the low attendance was to rename the Sacrament. It's new name was the Sacrament of Reconciliation. The church was trying to make the sacrament more appealing; of course, the tight little black boxes of the past didn't help. You didn't see many young people in line at confession. It was an old person's sacrament.

However, though young, I could feel the healing power of the words of absolution. It strengthened me to try again. Of course I would fail again, but the power was in never giving up. At least that was my take.

Non-Christians called Catholics hypocritical; or perhaps misguided. The forgiveness of sins without a change of behavior meant nothing. The people would be forgiven but continue to practice the same sins for years. I understood how the non-believers would call Catholics hypocritical. However, many Catholics did change. It might take years for certain sins; but it always gave me a feeling of starting fresh, clean.

The idea was to never give up; keep trying, don't give in. Perfection was elusive; but Jesus gave us the command to try.

The ability to restart my life was always life giving; a miracle of most sacraments.

I only hoped Manuel knew what he was doing. I took a deep breath. I knew this wasn't going to be just about masturbation. This was going to be intense.

CONFESSION

I walked straight up to Manuel and tried to get started, "Relax, there's no black box, nothing between us; just you and me. How long since your last confession?"

Manuel responded, "Almost 15 years, Father. You have to help me get through this."

I came back, "Of course, God doesn't care about the format we use. We can stumble through the prayers together. God only cares about what's in our heart. Okay, fifteen years. Are you now truly sorry for these sins you're about to confess?"

Manuel stared at the ground and said, "Yes Father. Very sorry."

"Okay. What sins do you want to reveal before God?" I couldn't believe it, I sounded like a priest.

Manuel took a deep breath. He looked me straight in the eye and said, "I have killed a man."

Silence.

"Yes, Manuel you have killed, anything else?" I tried to stay calm.

"Yes. I have committed adultery, sex with many women. Father, I have tortured people, hurt them bad. I have stolen. Father Adams, I have broken every commandment." Manuel dropped his head as he finished.

"Every commandment?" I asked as I reviewed them quickly in my head.

"But you must love God or you wouldn't be doing this Manuel."

Manuel thought for a second and replied, "I have faith. But I am weak. Plus this job; I'm asked to do bad things. I also do drugs and I'm probably an alcoholic."

I thought about what to say and spoke, "So you're human. You're a police man trying to catch bad guys. It's your job. However, killing is always wrong. Hurting people is not okay. Do you have children?"

"Yes Father, one young child, a girl. I love her but I don't live with her." Manuel seemed like he was finished.

I put my hand on his shoulder and said, "So there is still love in your heart. Is there anything else?"

"Yes, Father, I masturbate a lot. Strong libido, I guess." Manuel finally looked up as he spoke.

I glanced back at Mike who was deep in prayer; probably saying the words of absolution. I froze for a second and then put both my hands on Manuel's head. I said, "Please kneel" I knelt beside him with my hands still on his head.

I said a full act of contrition for Manuel. Then I pulled his head up and said, "You were brave to do this. Your sins are forgiven you in the name of the Father and of the Son and of the Holy Spirit. Go and sin no more."

Manuel answered, "Amen."

I looked him in the eyes and finished, "Manuel do not kill again. Do not torture or hurt anyone. Tell Eber what I said. He can give you a job that doesn't involve killing or torture. Don't be so self-destructive, drugs, alcohol, we are only meant to be addicted to the Word of God. Treat women with respect. For your penance, say ten Hail Mary's, ten, Our Father's, and give your daughter a big sober hug. She is your life." Manuel's eyes teared as I finished.

"Thank you Father Adams, you are a great priest." Manuel turned and ran from the plane.

I waved and ran around to the front of the plane and motioned to Mike that we could leave. We jumped into our seats and did the fastest pre-flight yet. We finally had a chance to escape. Mike turned the plane and headed out of the hanger. He glanced over at me and said, "Was it masturbation?"

I smiled and said, "Yeah, you were right. Are not priests sworn to a veil of secrecy on confession?"

"Yes." He replied, "but you're not a priest."

"I was for a few hours. It's not a bad gig." I laughed.

THE TRUTH

The flight over the border released any tension still residing in our bodies. American airspace felt warm and cozy. Our destination; San Luis Obispo. Four hour flight. I hoped my bladder could handle the length of this trip.

We left Mexicali late, so we had to fly over three hours at night to make it to San Luis Obispo. Our conversation quickly turned to the events of the morning, our masquerade.

I started. "Mike. We were actually lucky the Federales found us before the drug cartel. The bad guys would have really hurt us."

Mike looked stunned. He shook his head and said, "You totally missed it! Those were the bad guys. They were masquerading as police. We were all playing a game."

I gave him another point of view, "The police car that turned on his lights and moved us to the hangar was real. Real lights and siren. Anyone at the airport could see what they were doing. They had to be the real police. However, maybe you're right. The Federales were the crooks."

"You mean the police; the bad guys?" Mike responded.

"Yes. The good guys were the bad guys. You had it right, Mike." I mentioned.

Mike came back, "Okay. The police are in on it. Eber, The boss, the men, Carlos, the fishermen, the hotel kitchen crew.

135

Nico, that's a lot of people. But they could all make it look like the Police simply raided a suspected drug carrying plane."

"Not Carlos!" I reacted.

Mike didn't flinch, "Carlos was in on it. Somehow, I suspect, he felt guilty about knowing this was happening to us. He was touched by God. He saved us. He didn't want us to get hurt. He risked his life for our well-being. Incredible how God works."

I was trying to piece it all together. "So this coke is being distributed in Mexicali by the Police?"

"Yes. It's a perfect sting. The people think the police are actually doing their job; but in fact, they are running a drug cartel. They can't get caught. The people that transport the drugs for them don't even know they have the drugs. Amazing. I wonder how many shipments they deal with a week?"

I thought Mike was on to something, "The boss is the godfather of the business."

"Maybe. Maybe just an actor. Rarely would the real boss be anywhere near the illegal games these people play. They all played their parts. We made things sticky for them by being Catholic priests. They couldn't touch us." Mike looked proud as he finished.

"They scared the hell out of me." I reminded Mike.

"Me too!" Mike agreed.

"We might not ever know the whole truth." I had to say it.

"Yeah. Probably never really know everything. I am just glad to be alive and healthy. I almost lost my hands; I would have never flown again. You see Nick, it pays to be a priest; sometimes." Mike smiled.

"The whole priest thing probably saved us, Father Cross. Could you please tell the Bishop when we get back that I'm a priest?" I joked.

"You got five years of training son. But I'm already impressed with your knowledge of Church history and Theology. You were perfect back there. Maybe you have a vocation!"

"I have a girlfriend." I tried to deflect Mike's inquires.

Mike was focused. We relived what happened over and over. At times, we felt like we knew what happened, at others, we still couldn't make sense of it all. It seemed like a lot of work for a little cocaine. However, at no risk.

I was getting tired and needed to stretch my feet. The night air gifted us with incredibly stable air. The smoothness of the ride was nothing like flying in the daytime. The lights below us were beautiful.

We were at 7,000 feet with just about an hour left in the flight when Mike turned and asked, "So did you like being Father Adams?"

I thought, hear we go again; vocation. "Yeah Mike, it has its advantages. I am alive. I did my first confession, blessed a bunch of thieves and murderers and I'm probably going to Hell for impersonating a Catholic priest."

"Nico, you did a great job, handling that whole situation." Mike came back "I loved the Jesuit part. Very nice touch!"

"If I really wanted to be a Priest I don't know what order I would join." I truthfully responded,

"The priest thing saved us Mike. Thanks."

Mike smiled and nodded. I'm sure he thought I was well on my way to becoming a Catholic priest. After all, we had been through so much. It was impossible to ignore the possibility of a vocation for me. Was this my invitation to becoming a priest?

The vacation had turned again to a discernment process for me. Still, when did a person know that he had a vocation? How would I know God was knocking on the door? I had always felt a call to service; but what kind of service? A teacher? A coach? A Catholic priest? I also felt a strong call to raise a family.

I certainly first heard God's call back in my altar boy days. My faith helped me survive puberty, high school and my young adult days. I was far from perfect but compared to what was going on around me; I was a saint. The 1970's destroyed some of my friends. Free love, drugs, cults, and new age theologies dominated my generation. Everyday, from seventh grade to high school graduation; someone tried to get me stoned.

I was lucky. My faith and athletics saved me. My sense of morality instilled in me a code of moderation. Certainly, I made poor choices along the way but come Sunday morning, I was back in church. I never gave up trying to be a good person; however, perfection had always eluded me.

Out of nowhere Mike asked, "Nick, have you ever tried cocaine?"

I hesitated, because I certainly did try it. I couldn't lie to Mike, "Yeah, I'm not very proud to say I have tried it."

"What does it do? Why is it so popular?" Mike questioned.

"It is a stimulant. It increases the central nervous system. Breathing up, heart rate up, blood pressure up. It also causes the brain to release endorphins; serotonin especially."

Mike looked puzzled, "What does serotonin do?"

"Serotonin activates the pleasure center of the brain. It makes you feel good!"

"Every time?" Mike looked at me.

"Every time." I shook my head. Energy, plus stimulating the reward center of the brain. A very lethal combination. You can see why it is so popular."

Mike had more questions, "How do you use it?"

I felt like a Health teacher, "You can inject it, snort it or take it in orally. You can also smoke it. I just learned all this at San Jose State. Pretty good school, don't you think?"

"You injected it!" Mike was getting emotional."

"No. Would never do that! I snorted it. Gave it a try. It really works. It scared me; you could fall in love with it and never stop." I wanted out of this conversation.

"What other drugs have you tried?" Mike was probing.

"Alcohol, pot, and coke. Pot is probably the best. Very relaxing. My father was probably an alcoholic so I've always been careful with my consumption. Pot is like drinking a couple glasses of wine; without the alcohol and coke is crazy. I would never do that stuff again." I was serious.

"I like my brandy." Mike was coming clean. "Other than that I've had no experience with anything really. I guess I lived a pretty sheltered life."

"I think you're doing great, Mike." I smiled and looked down above San Diego.

We continued to talk about how many drugs the cartel could move from La Paz to Mexicali. They had a fool-proof scam: the guns, the uniforms, the authority to do whatever they wanted. In the end, we fell into a trap, escaped, and had a great story to tell.

After a great landing in San Luis Obispo we met up with Mike's friends who put us up for the night. I was exhausted; we had been through so much. We shared our stories and drank red wine. Just one more leg in our journey and we would be home. It was a wonderful thought.

YOUTH MINISTER?

Mike's friends dropped us off at the airport; their hospitality was never ending. They wined us and dined us and put us up overnight. They were astonished by our stories about what had happened. I couldn't believe we were less than four hours from home.

We quickly prepared the plane for take-off and soared into the air. Soon, we would be back at our starting point: Watsonville. Mike climbed the Archer II to 7,000 feet and leveled the plane out. Smooth air; just the way I liked it. I was calm, anxiety that was born on the earlier flights was gone. I finally felt I was going make it home safe.

My mind wandered to the responsibilities I would face when I got home. I had a girl- friend to check in with. I would start classes at San Jose State in two weeks. I was in the process of getting my teaching credential. My Bachelors of Science would be in Physical Education. One year of student teaching; a few classes to finish and I would have my credential. I also had minors in History, Health Science and California History. My life was full and moving fast. My dream of becoming a teacher was achievable; andwithin my reach.

However, Father Mike was about to blow all that up. He put the plane on auto-pilot and turned towards me. He sighed and said, "Nick, there is something I want to talk to you about."

Mike continued but raised his voice, "This isn't about the trip. I want you to be my Youth Minister, next year."

I knew Mike had a well liked youth minister; he seemed to draw a lot of kids to the youth group meetings. "Mike, why change? You have a good youth minister."

Mike responded, "Yes, I know this. You have a better background in Theology, Church History and Tradition. Besides, you have a college degree. You're a teacher!"

"Yes, but Ministry is different. Mike I quit the youth group at St. Joseph's when I was fifteen; it sucked. It wasn't working. Everyone quit."

Mike was fast to speak, "Okay. You know what doesn't work; then do something that works!"

What Mike said challenged my faith. I felt Jesus was asking me to be his youth minister. I loved working with high school kids. A full time youth minister sounded good to me. I was beginning to process the possibilities. I could still have a girl-friend, a wife or whatever I wanted. School would have to be put on hold; this was a life changing decision. My mind tried to envision all the possible timelines. All the problems. I was trying to talk myself into this. Still, it was crazy. I was ready to turn down Mike's proposal when some foreign incarnate power grabbed me. I turned to Mike and said, "Okay. I'll be your Youth Minister. I will commit to one year at a time. Hey, what's it pay?"

"I don't know. I'm guessing; a couple thousand." Mike answered.

"A month? A couple thousand a month?" I needed information.

"A year! Come on! Are you kidding. But you also get room and board. You can live in the rectory. You can eat with us priests. I will give you a gas card. Is this sounding better?"

Mike answered every inquiry I had about the job. He assured me his current youth minister could finish the year; I would start in the summer of next year.

Then, another unexpected gift came from Mike voice. "Nick, I want to send you the Emmaus Training School for Youth Ministers. It lasts almost the entire summer. This training school is one of the best in the land. Outstanding teachers. You will live there and study with over 40 other students. They teach theology, church history, and running a youth group. You will come back as a fully trained Youth Minister; ordained by Bishop Quinn of San Francisco."

"Ordained?" I was already on edge. "Are you kidding me?"

Mike laughed and said, "Sorry wrong word. You'll be commissioned; not ordained."

"No vows. Right?" I quickly stated.

"Oh, no vows. No No. No." Mike couldn't say no enough. "So, what do you say? Are you in?"

I couldn't believe what was being offered. Theology, church history. Working with the youth. A giant leap of faith was now required on my part. My life plans would be greatly changed I again felt the spirit inside me.

I confidently responded, "Yes Mike. I'll go to Emmaus. I'll be trained as a youth minister. I will live at the rectory and eat breakfast and dinner with the priests living there. I will make St. Joseph's Church the best youth group in the diocese. However, I have a request. I want to continue coaching at the local high school in the afternoons."

Mike was again ahead of me, "Coaching at the high school will let you on the campus. You can easily reach our kids there. Campus Ministry is part of your job description. If you have time be a substitute teacher; that's even better. You could have lunch with kids. The contact at the school is something I can't do; a youth minister could. Nick you will be involved in our religious education program too! We have a director but you be like a co-director. She can take grades 1-6 and you do the junior high and high school. You can do Confirmation too! Heck, you would be the only credentialed teacher we have."

"Mike this sounds like a big job! In fact, it sounds like lots of jobs!" I was concerned.

Mike slowed down and reminded me, "Let's let the Emmaus School deal with the whole job description. You are a teacher. You're way ahead of the game."

"Okay, you get a credentialed teacher next year. I start the job in August. I'm excited!" I couldn't believe how my life was changing.

Mike added more work. "I almost forgot. Could you put together a band and play music for the 9 am youth mass?"

"Wow. Stop!" I spoke loudly. What are you going to do?" I joked.

"We will be a good team. Just like this trip. I guarantee you Nick. You will love the work. And besides, you've already been a priest. A youth minister should be nothing."

When Mike asked me to be his youth minister I was stunned. Mike had every answer to all my questions. A spiritual door was opening right in front of me. A door I didn't knock on.

Time stood still. Jesus seemed to be talking right through Mike. This was my invitation to be a builder of the kingdom. Jesus, incarnate. My ears heard Jesus talk. This revelation overwhelmed me. I was learning that Jesus was in people. Father Mike, Carlos, Eber, everyone.

Jesus must be in all of us, the good, bad, old and young. It was like an extra sense for those who believed. I never felt it so strong. It was crazy. Would I really turn my life totally around? Was this my vocation moment to the priesthood?

I turned to Mike and said, "I'll go to Emmaus. I'll do something that works. I'll be a youth minister."

"I know." Mike said confused. "You accepted the job twenty minutes ago. Are you okay?"

"Sorry. This is all very intense." I snapped out of my day dream.

Mike smiled. "It's okay. The parish will love you."

"Yea, but I hope we don't have a mutiny when you get rid of your youth minister. It will be quite awkward." I pointed out.

"Let me take care of that. You just get trained." Mike stated.

The rest of the flight crawled by as we were both anxious to get home. We were 30 minutes from touch down when the weather cooled and the sky turned dark below us. A huge blanket of fog covered the land in front of us and seemed to go on forever.

I looked at Mike and could feel his concern. All he said was, "Fog."

BLACK FOG

Our starting point at the beginning of this vacation was Watsonville, California. It is found in the middle of the flattened horseshoe shaped Monterey Bay. At one end, is Monterey, with its world famous. Pebble Beach. It is arguably one of the most beautiful spots in the golf world, maybe the whole world. And at the other, is Santa Cruz, with its world class attraction the Boardwalk. It had one of the oldest Roller Coasters in the world, also one of the best.

Watsonville was directly in between, an agricultural sweat-box filled with migrant workers and artichoke fields. An economy run on hourly wages, strong backs, and greedy owners. Migrant workers flocked to Watsonville to find a job and start a new life. The Spanish language was alive in Watsonville and gave hope to generations of workers.

No one vacationed in Watsonville. However, I couldn't wait to see Watsonville's airport. Mike also had to turn the plane over to another co-owner. Mike later told me there were three different owners.

Mike called friends, family and my mom from San Luis Obispo just before we took off. He wanted a large welcoming committee for us; we deserved it.

The Monterey Bay also had a weather feature in late August: fog. At times, it acted like an air-conditioner. Other times, it blocked the blue sky for weeks sending the entire community into a mild depression. The fog could also get thick. Visibility could be challenging; even on the ground. Usually, the fog lifted about noon, and returned when the sun went down. Grey in color, it cooled even the hottest day and refreshed the stale sizzling air. Some people liked it; some hated it. I always liked it.

However, those feelings were being tested. From three thousand feet above the fog, it looked dark and ominous. The color seemed black as smoke. The fog was thick and gave us no clue as to where the ground actually was.

We reached the outskirts of Salinas; the sky was clear but thick fog was visible in front of us. We only had twenty minutes left but we would have to dive into the fog to land. The line of fog covered the entire Monterey Bay. There were no breaks anywhere along the coast line. Mike frowned and tried to deflect any anxiety I might already have. "Nick. We'll have to do an instrument approach. I am certified for radar landings. I've done this many times. Don't worry. If you want I can land here, in Salinas. You've been through a lot; instrument landings can be rough."

I couldn't believe it. Back straight into another stressful situation. I wanted safety; I wanted to end the drama. However, I had to finish with Mike; landing in Salinas felt like running away. Giving up. I told Mike, "Let's land in Watsonville. Everyone is waiting for us there. You have to turn over the plane to your friend; he's waiting. Show me how good you are at instrument landings."

Mike's face lit up with confidence. He immediately tried to explain to me what forces we would be up against. "Okay. Nico, when we break into the fog, visibility will be zero. I need to find my vector; an electronic signal sent from the ground that the plane catches. It tells us where we are. We make two left turns and drop out of the fog and land the plane."

It sounded so simple but when we lowered the plane into the fog all I could see was black. It was as if someone painted dull black paint all over our window's. This sensation overwhelmed me. We were totally at the mercy of the planes instruments.

I hated the feeling of not being able to see where we going. I became disoriented immediately. Instant nausea. We were blind.

Mike made contact with the tower and asked clearance for landing and wanted some information about the conditions on the ground. I thought the conditions were horrible. An air traffic controller gave Mike some directions and said visibility was good once you broke 300 feet.

Mike finished the conversation, "Still trying to catch vector, will advise."

My eyes caught site of sweat building on Mike's upper lip. Once again my pilot was being squeezed by stress. He seemed uncomfortable. Anxious. He made a few turns, said a few swear words; he couldn't find the vector. I had visions of crashing into a mountain side, or a building.

Mike fiddled with knobs on the control panel and didn't get the result he was looking for. Again a few more turns. Where were we? Flying in complete blackness challenged all my senses. My equilibrium was now completely distorted. I couldn't feel if we were going up or down. Left or right had no meaning.

Panic ensued "Mike, where are we?"

"Somewhere above the Watsonville airport, I hope. I should be getting these readings but I think I've just been circling the airport."

"Okay, we don't really know where we are. Could we be out over the bay. Over the water?" I felt we could be anywhere.

Mike stuttered, "This is the thickest black fog I've ever seen. I should be able to do this. I'm frustrated. But yes, to answer your question, it's possible we could be over the bay."

Suddenly we hit an air pocket and dropped violently. Mike mumbled some words but finished with, "Dear Jesus help me!"

I yelled, "Say what. Dear Jesus? Are we in trouble?"

"Nick calm down. I just can't find that dam vector. I am not exactly sure where we are. This fog is crazy!" Mike raised his voice.

"Okay Mike. Take me back to Salinas. No fog there. No drama there. I can't take any more of this. I can feel my heart pounding through my chest. Climb above the fog now!"

Mike didn't hesitate, "You're my co-pilot, good idea. I know how to do that."

He climbed the plane out of the fog and leveled us off. We did a quick check to see where we were and indeed found we were over the bay. He banked hard left and pointed the plane south to Salinas. My senses welcomed being able to see where we were going.

Mike patted me on the back and said, "Fifteen minutes Nico, I'll grease the landing in Salinas. You will be walking on the soil in no time. Of course, I'll have to go back. The plane needs to be in Watsonville and I can do that instrument landing. Besides, we have people waiting to see us. Nick I've got to do this as a pilot. I can't be scared of anything. It could save my life."

I jumped in, "It could kill you too!"

"Not on this trip. I would have been dead a long time ago." Mike repeated, "Not on this trip."

I didn't like his idea of flying back alone. I understood

his resolve as a pilot, but it seemed too risky. After a smooth landing Mike dropped me off at the Salinas Airport. I tried to talk him out of going back. I felt it was too dangerous. "Mike, if anything happens to you, I would have a tough time with that."

"Come on. Come on. Have some faith. I have done instrument landings over Watsonville, many times. I can do it." Mike, on the other hand, was stubborn. Father Cross had to land the plane in the fog.

"Is there anything I could say to talk you out of this?" I said.

"Nope. I should be back here in about 45 minutes, if everything goes okay." Mike said good humorlessly.

"Not funny. I will be praying; be aware of that. Mike, I should be going with you!"

"No no. You have had enough! No more talking." Mike motioned for me to shut the door.

I watched him take off and I headed straight for the bar. In some ways I hoped I didn't let him down. In others, I just wanted to drink. Nothing felt good about this. My self-esteem evaporated. Each breath was a struggle. The pace of my breathing quickened as I sucked as much air in as I could. Long exhales interrupted my attempts at slowing everything down.

I couldn't remember praying while gulping down beer but it seemed the thing to do. Prayers and beer: a new concept. The more I drank the more I prayed. Just one more hurdle to jump. He couldn't crash and burn now; too much was at stake.

BACK AT THE BEGINNING

I sipped my beer thinking about Father Mike. What did he have to go through to land the plane in Watsonville? Why did he have to challenge himself? He was safe on the ground in Salinas. Certainly, all our friends could have driven to Salinas.

The next hour and a half was about beer and prayer. Mike told me he could be back to Salinas in less than two hours. He just had to turn the plane over to his partner. I was almost feeling like I abandoned him. This whole trip would change into a nightmare if anything happened to Mike. My mother was one of the people waiting in Watsonville. If she saw Father Mike without me, she would freak out.

My mind tried to explore all the possible obstacles Mike would have to deal with. It just felt awkward not being with Mike. I felt uneasy, like I wimped out. Right at the end, I chickened out. I was so brave for so long, now I felt like a coward. I should have stayed with him. Where was the brave Father Adams? Where was my courage? Where was my faith? I abandoned my friend. I let him go back into a dangerous situation alone.

My self esteem was wilting by the second. I wished I were with him but all I could do was wait. I wanted to triumphantly walk off the plane together to the cheers of our friends and family. Instead, I sat alone in the Salinas airport bar feeling sorry for myself.

Less than 45 minutes had passed when I got bored and looked out the window of the bar to the landing aircraft. I probably watched five planes land when I noticed something very familiar about the sixth plane. It looked like the Archer II. One man was flying it and it was Father Cross. I figured the fog was too much for him and he returned to Salinas. I didn't care; I was happy to see him alive and well. We could finish the trip together.

I raced out to the tarmac to meet the plane. Mike waved and motioned for me to get in the plane. On the passenger seat was Mike's dog; Charlie. A small black terrier sitting on his back feet and looking out the window.

"Move over Charlie," Mike yelled.

Before I sat down I asked Mike, "What's going on? Dogs can fly?"

Mike smiled, "I landed in Watsonville; piece of cake. I talked to your Mom, everything's fine. I have some friends from the parish there too. Anyhow, I was just getting ready to drive to Salinas when the fog started lifting. We have over a mile of visibility now. I decided to fly to Salinas because it's faster."

I came to the truth, "I'm so glad we can finally land in Watsonville, together!" I asked him to forgive me for being such a coward.

"Father Adams. You are one of the bravest friends I have. You are anything but a coward." We laughed and took off straight for Watsonville.

Mike explained, "Your mother said you did the right thing by asking to go to Salinas. I told her we would never take any chances. Safety first was always our top priority with you." Mike tried to hold back his laugh but it burst through his lips.

I was already laughing. My mom would be shocked from what we were about to tell her.

Mike continued, "Now, most of all, I'm glad we're going to land together."

"Me too!" I shot out.

Landing in Watsonville with Mike erased all my disappointment. It turned me around to experience joy, relief, and happiness. I just flew with Mike's dog, Charlie, on my lap from Salinas to Watsonville. I asked Mike if dogs were allowed on aircraft. "Mike doesn't this break some kind of rule?"

"Probably, but that's not your biggest problem. You know, he hasn't gone to the bathroom in a while. He kinda has that look, you know." Mike's eyes got real big.

I looked at Charlie and told him he could make it. My waving arms singled Mike to hurry to park the plane. I could see our welcoming committee. I patted Mike on the arm and we exchanged eye contact. I needed to say one final thing, "Thank you, Mike. Great pilot! Great friend!"

Mike accepted my comment with warmth. He cut the engines and reached over and gave me a hug. "You're the best co-pilot ever. Now let's get out of here, there is a party waiting for us!"

We made it.

AFTERTHOUGHTS

In the end, we flew over 3,000 miles. We took off twelve times and landed, thank God, twelve times. The "vacation" lasted sixteen days. The plane gulped down 240 gallons of fuel; only once were we low on our reserve tank. Mike always made sure we had enough fuel. He tested the fuel, and was a confident, well qualified pilot. I believe his skill and composure saved our lives more than once.

Our top cruising speed was 120mph and we could fly between 5,500 and 7,500 feet. Mike, over his career, ended up with over 3,500hrs of flight time and two trips across the United States. Of course, he had one remarkable trip to Cabo San Lucas.

The trip started on July 20th, 1980 and we returned back on Aug. 6th. We started from Watsonville, California and flew as far south as Cabo San Lucas. We traveled further south to Mazatlan, and in between, we landed the Piper 180, Acher II in San Luis Obispo, Calixico, Mexicali, San Felipe, La Paz, Cabo San Lucas, Loretto, Catavina, and Watsonville.

I was 21 in 1980 and Mike was 45. He had been a parish priest for many years. He had spoken of taking the Bishop up in his plane. His office is littered with pictures of his planes and the trips that they took. It always made him smile.

Today, July 6th, 2012, almost 32 years after our incredible

adventure, Mike and I have aged. In fact, Mike has celebrated his 50 year anniversary to the priesthood. Now in his 70's, he is semi-retired, still ministering to a small parish, St. John's in Felton, California. I was blessed to attend his 50 year anniversary Mass. The Bishop attended, as well as many priesthood friends and family.

I always felt I owed him so much; he probably saved my life. He believed in me; made me a youth minister, a job I held for five wonderful years. He also taught me to trust in God and forgive everyone.

I glanced around the dining room as a beautiful luncheon manifest itself, a tribute to Father Cross's great life so far. Mike sat with the Bishop, and some priest friends. The walls had pictures of some of Fr. Cross's great adventures.

Mike took one trip a year whenever he could. The walls, peppered with pictures from 30 or 40 years back, showed different planes, and different places that Mike visited. I really had to search for the Piper 180, Archer II. It had green racing strips down its side and wheel fenders.

Finally, I found the plane on the back wall. I started thinking about the trip. I bet many of these people could tell stories of past experiences with Mike. I was just one of many.

The rest of the luncheon we all told stories of Mike's adventures. Really incredible stuff. I felt lucky to have been one of them. I would always have my story; so would Mike. We had been getting together occasionally for dinner to talk about old times.

Looking back on our lives we realized we lived a remarkable event between us. A bonding event. Mike had aged well. On the other hand I was now 53. Married for 25 years, and now divorced. Living alone in Capitola, on the Monterey Bay. I am blessed to have two children, Aaron, who just turned 21 and Sara, who just cracked 16.

I was hoping for a forever marriage but it didn't work out. At first, angry feelings toward God surfaced, but I thought back to this trip and how God helped us to survive.

Divorce was horrible. A humbling experience. However, I gained strength from knowing God was right where he wanted me to me. I don't know how or why, but I am right where God wants me. He is still looking out for me and guiding me. Hopefully I can engage in more adventures.

I have good days; bad days too, like everyone else. Fifty three years is a true blessing: children who love me, good health, strong faith and a will to help others.

It was good to reconnect with Mike when I started writing this book. We laughed aloud again in telling or retelling the stories in the book. Father Cross would call me a survivor, still alive, and still kicking. He told me God still had some work for me. He mentioned becoming a deacon, priest, or brother. He had never quit on me having a vocation.

I have been one lucky man; a youth minister, teacher, coach, musician, and writer. Mike gave me new realities, new possibilities. Mike was a good friend and touched so many people.

One, night we were eating at a restaurant and a couple of Mike's parishioners recognized Mike and came up greet him. He introduced me as "Father Adams". He did this all the time.

I smiled and followed that with a glare. I whispered to Mike, "That isn't true. Stop that."

Mike would always respond, "Oh yes it is. You have two kids!" I just shook my head.

Today, I was reminiscing about our experiences. Mike downplayed everything that happened to us. I was glad we had remained friends. The last thing Mike told me as we hugged and departed was, "Nico, you were the best co-pilot I ever had. Our trip was really just a piece of cake."

Mike held up his hands, stared at them, and motioned them back and forth. "I love my hands Nico!"

We both erupted into laughter.

ACKNOWLEDGMENTS

Thank you to Father Mike Cross who reached out in friendship to a parishioner and offered the adventure of a lifetime. You did "get us back" eventually. Friends for life.

Thank you, Dane Paulson, who said, "You might have something here!" after reading the early versions of Father Adams. Your inspiration kept me going.

Thank you Becky Armor, for giving me ideas, editing, and pumping me up. Actually, I think you liked Fr. Cross's character more than mine. I do too!

Thank you, Geoffrey Dunn, author, historian and friend. I admire your talent so much.

Thank you, Aaron Adams, for formatting and organizing my manuscript. You got it where it had to go. Love you!

Thank you, Sara Adams, for believing in me and inspiring me to keep working. Love you!

Thank you, Joseph Allegri, for helping me format the chapters and being such a great friend.

Thanks to all my friends who kept pushing me to "get this done" I am blessed to have had such loving relationships. God has truly blessed me. Amen.

I had a plane yesterday!

Ho-hum, just another trip to Baja.

Has anyone seen my plane?

Someone stop that plane, it's mine!

Oh no, where's my blow dryer?

I love my plane!

Don't worry Nick, the odds are with us.

You can't get me to sit in there. I'll just stand on the wing.

Are you sure we're going the right way?

Nick have you ever landed on a dirt field?

This doesn't look like a gas station!

Hi mom, we are in Cativina

Our welcoming commity.

Maria is on the left.

Mike doesn't the plane look a little tired?

Does anyone know where the good water is?

I'm so proud of this baby.

How high did you say we are?

Over-crowded beaches are everywhere.

They seemed to know we were coming.

Love those pools, say bartender.

I told ya we'd make it to Matzalan. But how do we get home?

Baja is rugged in some places, living is tough.

Just one more picture.

Some days you just feel ten feet tall.

What a life.

What did you say the odds were?

What a plane.

Charley, not on the wing!

Two skybuddies, who beat the odds; what an adventure!

Printed in the United States
By Bookmasters